THE DEFENDING HEART

Judy Henderson finds herself in the wrong place at the wrong time on three fateful occasions. She witnesses her first employer fall out of her window, and her second employer she discovers dead at the foot of the stairs. Then there's the nurse she sees pushed off a train. Dr David Marland is the only person who believes Judy's fantastic tales — and how is her enigmatic boyfriend involved? Together, Judy and David must uncover the terrifying truth that links the deaths — before more are added to the list . . .

Books by Delia Foster
in the Linford Romance Library:

TREASURE OF LOVE
ROMANCE AT ST. ELNA
MASTER OF THE ISLAND
STRANGER IN THE FOG
THE CAMWORTH CAMEO
WILLIAM'S WIFE
CASUALTY PATIENT
FUGITIVE NURSE

SPECIAL MESSAGE TO READERS

THE ULVERSCROFT FOUNDATION
(registered UK charity number 264873)

was established in 1972 to provide funds for research, diagnosis and treatment of eye diseases. Examples of major projects funded by the Ulverscroft Foundation are:-

- The Children's Eye Unit at Moorfields Eye Hospital, London
- The Ulverscroft Children's Eye Unit at Great Ormond Street Hospital for Sick Children
- Funding research into eye diseases and treatment at the Department of Ophthalmology, University of Leicester
- The Ulverscroft Vision Research Group, Institute of Child Health
- Twin operating theatres at the Western Ophthalmic Hospital, London
- The Chair of Ophthalmology at the Royal Australian College of Ophthalmologists

You can help further the work of the Foundation by making a donation or leaving a legacy. Every contribution is gratefully received. If you would like to help support the Foundation or require further information, please contact:

THE ULVERSCROFT FOUNDATION
The Green, Bradgate Road, Anstey
Leicester LE7 7FU, England
Tel: (0116) 236 4325

website: www.foundation.ulverscroft.com

DELIA FOSTER

THE DEFENDING HEART

Complete and Unabridged

LINFORD
Leicester

First published in Great Britain in 1977

First Linford Edition
published 2019

A catalogue record for this book is available
from the British Library.

ISBN 978–1–4448–4193–0

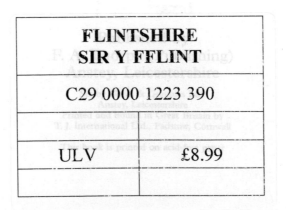

1

The watery sunshine burst through one of the not very clean windows of No. 17, Highview Avenue, and touched Judy Henderson's pale hair to gold. It was like a shining halo, old Miss Remington thought. Like everything else about her secretary-companion, it was elusive yet fascinating. You wouldn't call the girl pretty, the old woman thought irritably, and yet she was irresistable to the local youth. From her window, she had watched the girl leave, at the end of the day, and male heads turned for that second look; at the frail pallor of her cheeks, or perhaps the rather withdrawn air which was somewhat unusual in young women these days? Judy wore no make-up, or hardly any. Her lashes were long and dark, under delicately marked dark brows, and the blue eyes were not exactly blue, more of a smoky violet. And with all that male interest, the only man the girl had eyes for, Miss Remington thought in some frustration, was that smooth young devil, who was always hanging around her; a young man the elderly spinster neither liked nor trusted.

'Why do you go on working for me?' she asked suddenly, startling Judy, so that she dropped her ball-point pen and had to search to see where it had rolled. 'Oh, never mind, take another out of the drawer,' Miss Remington snapped. 'My fault, but there's no call to get your clothes dusty. Everything here is dusty. No one to do the housework. And no, I wouldn't like you to take on my house cleaning as well as everything else you do for me. I can't think why you stay here. Why don't you go and work in a smart office, where there's a lot of other young people, and a decent typewriter, and nobody as old as I am around? Why do you want to put up with an old woman like me?'

Judy smiled, a sudden dazzling smile like a sunburst after a shower. 'You don't want to get rid of me, do you? Then don't let's talk about it. I like working for you.'

'Yes, but why? What does your family think about it?'

Judy hesitated. 'Miss Remington, I've been with you for three months. Aren't you satisfied with me? I told you at the start that I have no family. I'm alone. I live in a boarding house.'

'And that — man-friend of yours — he lives there too?'

'Yes.' Judy's colour was heightened. Her heart began to beat faster. She was well aware that Miss Remington had never liked Noel, though the old lady would never say why. Well, he was smooth. He did like to get his own way. His bossiness was somewhat frightening at times; it worried Judy, the way she gave in and let him over-ride her, especially with the matter of talking about the old lady's business. Noel always said that if they were going to be married, surely there was some trust between them and she could tell him everything? And he was so possessive. Could Miss Remington see that, too, and did she object?

'My dear,' Miss Remington said, on a softer note, 'you have the sort of face that gives away everything. I can tell at this moment that you are thinking I am a nosey old busybody and that it might all well have been left unsaid. But I worry about you. Do you know that?'

'Why should you?' Judy asked, in surprise.

'I don't know. I worry about a lot of things.' Miss Remington seemed to shrink a little, and then she straightened her back, seemed to pull herself together, and said firmly, 'Not true! I do know why I worry about you. You look so . . . well, I know I can trust you, but I don't know what your background is. It's this house. Too big for me. I am not a coward, but I do worry because I can't get someone to come in to clean it up, and to be here — no matter how much I offer them, no one will come.' She hesitated, met Judy's politely enquiring look, and gave a dry chuckle. 'You're right, I don't offer them the earth. No use. They wouldn't do one scrap more work if I offered them double. They don't like work nowadays. Well, all right then, they don't like cleaning up a large cluttered inconvenient old-fashioned house like this one. There! Now I've said it, and you and I both know it's the truth, but nothing can be done about it. I've thought about going to some other place but where would I go?'

'Go to a hotel, a small cosy one — '

'Is there such a thing?' Miss Remington snorted. 'Besides, there'd be other people my age, who'd want to talk, pry into my affairs. No, I like being alone. Besides, how would I keep my birds, and the animals, in a hotel?'

That was an irrefutable point. Judy sighed. There was a mynah bird in a cage, and a pair of budgies long past their first youth. They always needed cleaning out, not a job Judy liked. There was the Peke, old and fat and snappy,

5

and the two elderly cats, pampered, and sour; too sour to even evoke an interest in the birds. Miss Remington said, 'My first love is the birds, of course. And who'll look after them when I'm gone?' she finished fiercely.

'Oh, don't talk like that!' Judy protested.

'It's got to be talked about, my dear.' Miss Remington, never good-looking, looked quite hideous for a moment, so ferocious was her face, and to judge by her eyes, her thoughts, too. 'You see, it used to be easy to think of how one would dispose of one's worldly goods. Personally, I mean. I knew what I had, and it was all to go — this house as well — to my pet charity, the society who looks after birds. Oh, where is that pamphlet about them — I never can remember their name. Oh, here it is. But the thing is, they don't look after cats and dogs, and my darlings need looking after too. And another thing, I used to know what I possessed, but now I don't. Either things get moved, or they vanish. I don't know.'

'What do you mean, Miss Remington?' Judy asked fearfully.

'Oh, don't sound so scared, child. I'm not accusing you. But the fact remains, I now have no daily help, since the last one took herself off, and last night I was downstairs looking for — well, never mind what. But it wasn't there. And I hadn't moved it. At least, I don't think I moved it.'

'Yes, you did, you old fool!' the bird said suddenly.

'Tell me what it is, and I'll help you look for it,' Judy suggested. 'No, I've got a better idea. How would it be if we started in to tidy your house? Go through it and make an inventory and throw out any rubbish and clean it up as we go? We haven't got so many letters to write as there were, and anyway, I can stop and do them at night, if you like.'

Miss Remington looked sharply at her. 'You mean that? You'd want paying! Don't say you wouldn't — I know better! And you'd be paid all right — of course you would. It would be your due! And I know you'd do the job thoroughly. Oh, I'm tempted.'

'Then why don't you say yes? I've been wanting to suggest a clean-up and throwing out of — some things I'm sure you have no more use for. Things like old packing and old envelopes and string — everyone collects them and everyone ought to have a turn out sometimes. Do let me help you!'

Miss Remington looked thoughtful. She wanted to say yes so badly, but at the back of her mind was the thought that someone else had prompted the idea. That young man of Judy's. Because he wanted to know what was there. Miss Remington was sure she had seen the shadow of a tall man against the frosted glass of the back door last night, against the light of the moon. Imagination? She wanted to believe that, so badly.

The thought reminded her of doors. 'Did you lock all the doors downstairs when you came up last time? Every door? Every window? No, don't say there's only the two of us here and it doesn't matter. It does! Rosie is too old a dog to protect us, and someone might get in. It's getting dark already!' She looked out at the greying scene; the blind eyes of unlighted windows in other buildings, and the forest of roofs and chimney-pots. Worse than living in the middle of a field, Miss Remington thought, because those buildings were either empty now or filled with empty faces, peering hostile eyes . . .

'Come, child, let me put my hand on your shoulder and we'll go down together and make sure everything's all right. Then you can make some tea and carry the tray up for me and we'll have it together. With that nice cake you bought for me on the way back from your lunch. You really are a very good child to me.' And the mynah bird screamed: 'That's right, leave me all alone!'

Judy would rather have skipped down the stairs and got round the checking of the entries to the house, alone. It was trying and a bit hazardous, going down-stairs at snail's pace with Miss Remington's hand biting into her shoulder, and the Peke and cats getting in the way: anxious to come but not willing to go first. It was as if they all expected an enemy to be in the house and were relying on Judy, the brave, the unbelieving, to prove them all wrong. The weight of their fear was almost a tangible thing.

'Do let me go down alone, Miss Remington. I'll get the tea and do the locks and you've no need to worry about a thing.'

'Well, I have, then! I have reason to believe that somebody gets in and robs me. There, it's out, and I feel better for saying so. And don't look like that, miss — as if you thought there was nothing in this house worth taking. There is! Come, I'll show you something,' and she diverged on the first landing to a room at the end, a dark musty-smelling room where she kept her Eastern treasures, all old and dreary, with dust all over them.

Fans, screens, joss stick burners, great embroidered panels hiding the walls — panels worked in wools and gilt threads, of hideous dragons and other symbols which Judy felt would give her nightmares if they belonged to her.

'Now, you might say to yourself that if there was anything of value in here, I would take it upstairs, keep it by my bed at night, where I would see it was safe, wouldn't you? And that is just what I expect outsiders to think.'

Miss Remington chuckled at her own cleverness, and leaned over a small Buddha, blotting out Judy's view of it. The old woman put out a hand, there was a click, and she moved back, to reveal a drawer that had shot out from the base of the statue. There, lying on a dingy bed of velvet, were scattered stones, it seemed to Judy, who couldn't get very close because of Miss Remington's body.

Miss Remington murmured, 'There! Nobody knows about that but you and me so if anything happens to it, I shall know I was wrong to trust you. Nobody but me knows how to work the secret drawer. That is why I blocked your view so that you shouldn't see how I opened it. Now look at it more closely.' She hooked a finger in among the stones and it came up slowly, a diamond necklace that fell into a handsome, if rather heavy and ornate, pattern as she held it high.

'Now, what do you think of that?' she asked Judy sharply.

'Frankly, and please don't be hurt, Miss Remington, I — well, it isn't my taste. I don't know the value of it but it must be worth a lot. Is it?'

'It's worth thousands,' Miss Remington said.

'Then why do you keep it here? Why don't you put it in the bank's vaults?'

'I never go out, so how could I? And don't suggest that I send for some young fool of a clerk from the bank, who would be stupid enough to show someone, or lose it or get run over or — oh, no, it stays here. Its been safe all these years and it will continue to be safe, until I pass on and my sole relative takes over.' She peered at Judy. 'I've altered my Will,' she said abruptly.

'Sole relative? I thought you were alone, Miss Remington. I thought . . . '

'What did you think?' the old woman asked sharply.

'I thought you and I were both alone in the world and it seemed to make a bond between us,' Judy said haltingly. 'Except . . . you've got animals, of course.'

'And you've got a man friend? Now I must require you to promise not to mention this to a soul — to nobody, nobody at all. You hear?'

Judy promised readily enough but she looked hurt. Was a promise necessary? 'I wish you'd come with me, in a taxi, with that, to the bank. The manager would take you to the vaults and you could see it put away safely,' Judy urged.

Miss Remington looked tempted. 'I'll see,' she said at last. 'Now, that big book on the table in the window. Fetch it to me, child, and I'll show you something else.'

Judy turned and threaded her way through the piles of junk to the window, and as she did so, she heard Miss Remington move. Putting the necklace back again, she thought with a sad little smile; while my back is turned. She really doesn't trust me.

Nothing in that room of so-called treasures looked of the slightest value or interest, though they spent twenty minutes in there. But at last Miss Remington agreed to go back upstairs to her room while Judy made the tea and took it up to her. And when she arrived, her employer smiled and said, 'I've come to a decision. We *will* go to the bank tomorrow, you and I, with that necklace. And when we come back, we will make a start on cleaning the place up and you shall make an inventory and take down the rubbish to be burnt in the yard. There! Now take that incredulous look off your face, child, which tells me you think I am an obstinate and intractable old woman.'

Judy protested, then caught her employer grinning. Miss Remington had a rather malicious grin and had teased Judy before. Just a part of her complex character; half fears for her safety and the safety of her pets and treasures; half disliking the rest of the world and distrusting it.

But now she was admitting to having a relative. Judy asked tentatively as she cut slices of cake and poured tea, 'This relative of yours, is he near at hand?'

'No, and it's not a he, it's a she. And that's all I'm saying, miss. It's all in the hands of my solicitor. It's all right and tight, that's if the fool carries out my instructions, which come to think of it, I very much doubt.'

Soon after that, Judy was told to put the lights on. She hated this part of the day, when the whole of the place was changed, filled with deep and sinister shadows. Not that she feared a break-in. She knew she had locked all the doors and fastened the windows securely, and before she left at the end of each day she put into position the ancient wood shutters and bolted them on the inside. The back basement window had iron bars outside it, anyway, and the front one was in an area, above which was a solid grating. She sighed. Miss Remington's fears were contagious, although Judy feared more the mysterious things brought back from abroad and the great hairy spiders that lurked behind unpacked boxes and piles of rubbish. She feared, too the fire risk for her old employer. The electric system was old and shaky. There were gas fires, too, and Miss Remington wasn't very careful with turning off the taps.

As she drew the curtains, she saw Noel waiting, propping up the lamp-post across the street, reading a newspaper. He gave no sign, but he must have been aware that the lights were going on up here, and that she was pulling the curtains. 'Is he there?' Miss Remington asked. 'As if you didn't know who I mean — that man-friend of yours. You know very well who I refer to!'

'It's a man! She's got a man!' the mynah bird screamed, then fell silent.

Judy turned to her employer. 'You did say once that you were glad he came to meet me, rather than that I should have to walk home alone in the dark.'

'So I did. Well, I wish it was anyone but him,' Miss Remington snapped.

It was a strange ending to an unsatisfying day. Judy was glad when she was at last allowed to go. As always after going out and slamming the street door behind her, she stood on the front step for an instant, listening in case Miss Remington was tempted, in her fears for her own safety, to slip the bolt behind the front door. If she did, Judy wouldn't be able to get in next morning, so well barricaded were the rest of the entrances. They had had arguments about it before, Miss Remington insisting that she could come down and let Judy in, Judy gently but firmly pointing out that if Miss Remington were to fall or become ill, she might not be able to get the front door opened. So at last Judy had a key. And she waited until she heard Miss Remington's retreating footsteps, back up the stairs. If course, Judy thought uneasily, as she watched Noel lower his newspaper and carefully fold it and tuck it under his arm while she crossed the road to him — there was nothing to prevent the frightened Miss Remington from coming down at a later time and bolting that front door, was there?

Now Judy was away from the house, and in the almost empty but well-lit street she just wanted to forget about Miss Remington. But curiously enough Noel wanted to talk about her.

'What did you do today, love?' he asked, taking her arm possessively.

'Nothing much,' she countered, but he protested that that wouldn't do. He wanted to hear all about everything. So she said, 'Well, I walked the bad-tempered Peke, and fed all the animals and cleaned out the bird cages and let the cats out and finally called them in. I went out for lunch and brought back a cake for tea — '

That was a mistake. 'Not out of your money, I hope!' he said quickly.

'The cake was chiefly for me, because I have a long time to wait for my evening meal,' Judy said wearily. 'Nothing else happened apart from the letters I typed, so let's talk about something else. Where are we going to eat?' and the matter of the diamond necklace slid right out of her mind.

It was the one night of the week when they usually ate out, and Noel liked to take her to odd little places he had discovered. Tonight, however, he said shortly, 'Funds are low, love. I suggest we go back to eat at Mrs. Venny's.'

'Oh, no, I don't want to eat at the house tonight,' she cried. 'Let it be my treat, if you're hard up. Go on, I'll stand us fish and chips. Well, anything for a change.' Tonight she shrank from the same remarks from the other residents of the boarding house, whose whole conversation during the meal was predictable, what there was of it, for usually they raced through the meal, in order to be first in the scramble for the most comfortable chairs near the fire in the sitting-room.

Noel protested, but finally agreed to each paying their own, and at last they settled for a sausage and mash house at the bottom of a quiet back street.

Tonight their windows were steamy and there was a curious intimacy in sitting at one of the eight small washable-topped tables. The hiss of the fat in which the onions were cooking sent out a somnolent sound, and the smells were delicious. Judy settled back and sighed.

'You haven't heard a word I've said for the last five minutes,' Noel complained.

She brought her thoughts back with a jerk. 'I'm listening, Noel!'

'I've been asking you if you've mentioned that matter to the old lady — about signing those papers? Well, it's to her advantage, not mine!'

Judy looked fussed. She thought she had managed to persuade Noel to drop that idea. 'Look, I don't understand what it's all about — '

'You don't have to, love,' he broke in, impatiently. 'Just trust me, and take her the papers tomorrow and ask her to sign them.'

'She won't, you know. She's very intelligent. She'd want to know what they were all about. She'd show them to her solicitor.'

He leaned forward with intensity. 'Then don't tell her, if it's going to worry her. Just slip them between the letters you give her to sign and she'll sign them all together. Run the signing too near to post time to give any leeway for argument.'

'I couldn't do that!' Judy gasped.

'Why not?'

She started to say that it wasn't honest, and surprised an unpleasant look in his eyes. It was gone in a moment, but it had been a warning. One didn't tell Noel that what he was suggesting wasn't honest. So she said appeasingly, 'She's the sort to examine everything before she signs it, and if she's made to think I would try to slip in something without her knowing it, I'd lose my job.'

'You'll lose your job if she hears what I've heard about you in the past, love,' he said, and again there was menace under his tones in spite of the endearment.

'What d'you mean?' Judy asked, frowning, but her pulse was beating a little faster. Noel looked as if he was on very safe ground. He was a stranger tonight.

'Another old lady, wasn't it? And she died, didn't she? Or have I got you mixed up with someone else?'

Now Judy was really afraid; not of what he had found out about her but how he had found it out, and why he should have wanted to. But she said quietly enough, 'That was a long time ago. I can't stop a person having an accident and dying, and what does it matter? No, Miss Remington didn't ask me for details of long past jobs I've had;

just the last one or two. She knows I work as a companion and in typing pools — whatever comes up.'

'Yes, and its my guess you made your story good, love, and she took you on because she'd taken a fancy to you. But what if she was written to about you and your old ladies. Several of them, weren't there? All short duration. She might just wonder why they are old people you choose to work for. She might wonder all sorts of things, the way *I'd* put it to her.'

'No, she wouldn't,' Judy said unwisely, 'because she doesn't like you.'

His eyes narrowed, then he laughed. 'Well, what are we talking about? Take the documents tomorrow, love, ask her to study them, and if she doesn't find anything in it for her, then no harm done. But try it out. For me!'

Almost mesmerised, Judy took them from him. They were in a plain envelope. She tucked it into her handbag, wondering why she should fear Noel so much in this and yet like his company so much at other times. She supposed wearily that it was because she was lonely, and glad to have someone of her own to go around with.

After the meal he took her down to the river and they walked companionably watching the water traffic, people walking, like themselves, and gradually he calmed Judy into a happier mood, until they stopped beyond the pool of light from a standard lamp and he kissed her. When Noel kissed, he gently but firmly turned her body to his and held her in a grip that gradually got closer, tighter, while his lips threatened hers with more passion than she was ready for; yet tantalisingly the threat never quite materialised, leaving her hot and wondering why she had feared more than the embrace finally gave. That was Noel; playing on her feelings, leaving her vaguely unsatisfied, yet at the same time shrinking from being satisfied by him.

When they finally went back to the house, he had talked to her about the papers he wanted signed, so that she now had a hazy idea that if she didn't do her best to persuade her employer to sign them she would be cheating Miss Remington out of something of advantage to her. And yet she couldn't persuade Noel to explain it to her in terms that she understood. He lost his patience, or appeared to, and she was afraid of his sullen moods. Life was empty enough without Noel being hateful to her.

She lay sleepless that night, vaguely disturbed by his love-making, even more disturbed by the things he had suggested — not only about the documents that needed signing but also about that other elderly employer of hers and of how Noel could have come by the information. Someone he knew in the agency that had got her the job? It had been another old spinster, and she had died really from a fall. A look of great fear had been on her face as she lay dead, Judy remembered, but then terror did fill the features when one fell to one's death at any age, surely? She had been leaning out of her window, trying to reach her little cat which was stranded on a ledge and too terrified to make the effort to return to her at the window. The old woman had lost her balance and fallen out. Judy hadn't been there. She had arrived soon afterwards. She lay in bed shivering, remembering what had happened in the following hours; the questions, the way the neighbours had looked at Judy. But the doctor had said that he had warned his old patient not to lean out of her windows as she hadn't a good head for heights. And so it had all blown over.

But now Noel had raised the point, as if there was some doubt. But how could it affect Judy, except . . . if Miss Remington, who was so nervous, heard that an old employer of Judy's had died in such a way, well, what could she say? Judy took herself to task for allowing Noel to scare her like that. It hadn't been Judy's fault. But, Judy thought with a shudder that tore through her leaving her very cold and uncertain, Noel had such a way of putting words together, he could make it seem that Judy had had a hand, however indirectly, in the old woman's death. If only Judy had told Miss Remington about her. But she hadn't. It had seemed common sense to merely say she took any job that turned up and sometimes these were in typing pools, and agencies where the typists were sent out to different jobs all the time. True, but not chronologically so.

She slept finally, a dream-filled sleep in which documents and signatures and old ladies falling, Noel at his most hateful, and Miss Remington filled with horror, were all doing the strangest things as in dreams, but the terror was none the less real. She awoke unrefreshed and very late. Noel had already departed for the day, as had most of the other people in the house, when Judy went down. Mrs. Venny said sharply, 'Breakfast is finished!' as if she thought Judy would demand some at this hour, although she was dressed for the street. Judy smiled ruefully. 'Sorry. Too late to eat, anyway,' and went out into the rain and the wind.

Her umbrella blew inside out, she hadn't enough cash for bus or taxi after last night, and she was miserably aware that there were those documents in her handbag. She decided she would say nothing about them until she had Miss Remington in a good mood, which she surely wouldn't be, once she saw the time. Miss Remington hated people to be late. And in her heart Judy knew that Miss Remington would not want to look at anything Noel wanted signed, whether he said it was to her advantage or not.

Judy walked through the pouring rain with increasing fears of a scene with her employer. All the things Miss Remington said last night sprang to Judy's mind; if she had been afraid of that dark empty house last night, what would she feel today, when Judy asked her to do something prompted by Noel, which was, in her heart, something tricky. Noel never had an 'idea' without there was a lot in it for him. Judy had asked him before now, if it was a Power of Attorney, or Share Certificates or what, but she could never pin Noel down to a straight answer, and a cursory glance at the documents this morning had told her nothing. She didn't understand legal language and this one seemed too involved for words, but she was quite sure that it wasn't to Miss Remington's advantage and that Miss Remington would be the first to think so and say so.

Suppose she just returned them to Noel, saying Miss Remington had refused to sign them? But then he would communicate with the old lady and tell that story about Judy's previous old employer who had died . . .

Noel had once said, 'You never stay long in a job, do you, love? Bit of an albatross, aren't you? Well, no, perhaps your employers just think you are. Perhaps you're just one of those persons with a jinx, or they think so . . . ' and he always left the thought trailing in mid-air, and then made love to her, to comfort her and tell her he had been joking, or didn't mean it, or some such thing. He could be such fun when he liked, but after he had gone, and Judy couldn't sleep, she would remember what he had said about her being a jinx.

At last she plodded through puddles to the door of Miss Remington's house and struggled to keep her umbrella up while she found Miss Remington's key. Her hand was visibly shaking as she put the key in the lock, though she couldn't have said why. The door wouldn't open at first. Had Miss Remington bolted it after all? No, she couldn't have done, for the door moved inwards a little. It was as if there was an obstruction there.

She pushed harder, and it gave a little, enough for her to squeeze through but it was as if something heavy was against the door. 'Miss Remington, it's me, Judy!' she called.

The house was peculiarly still, as if it were empty. When her eyes got used to the gloom, she saw a movement at the top of the stairs. It would be Miss Remington shrinking back into the shadows.

Judy went forward, and almost fell over something in her path. How she regained her balance, she didn't know. And then she stood staring at the floor, unbelieving. Staring, staring, until suddenly a scream was torn from her throat. Miss Remington lay there, with the same look of horror on her face that Judy's other employer had had from her fall from the window. Miss Remington's feet were towards the stairs, and she was quite dead.

2

Blind terror filled Judy. It was like living over again that other job she had, when her employer had fallen from that upper window. Only that had been the first job in which an accident had happened. This was the second, a fact which Noel would be at pains to remind her.

Noel . . . she felt cold inside. Now she remembered that movement upstairs, when she had first come in. Who was it? Someone was here. The house hadn't an empty feeling, which it should have done. And where were the animals? Not a sound broke the stifling silence.

The animals . . . Dreading heaven knew what, Judy forced herself to go up the dark stairs. As she went, she cried, 'Is anyone there? Who is it up there? I know you're there!' Silly things to say, in a voice that didn't sound like her own.

Near the top, a sudden cold draught cut down across her face, with a musty odour to it, indescribably. She had never noticed such a thing in that stuffy unaired house before. A window open? But where would it lead to? Her heart banged suffocatingly against her ribs as she thought of cat burglars (climbers, she had once read they were called) who shinned up a drain-pipe and went into a window that might appear inaccessible to the average person.

Frenziedly she opened doors and looked briefly at windows, and having inspected each room's window, shutting the door carefully behind her. All the windows securely fastened from the inside, just as she had left them last night. Finally, she reached the room where she had been sitting with Miss Remington at tea yesterday, and there the fat old Peke lay, stiff, cold, dead. But not a mark on it. Poor old Rosie. No violence, she must have had a heart attack. She was old and much too fat. Miss Remington had often said so. But where were the cats? The silence of the birds was explainable. They had not been uncovered. That was the first thing Miss Remington did each morning, and she had probably let the cats out, and had not had time to let them in, before she — what? Fell down the stairs to her death? Passionately Judy wanted to believe that it was as simple as that. But there was the shadow of a person she had seen at the top of the first flight of stairs . . .

Yet when she had finished searching she was forced to admit to herself that there was nobody else in the house. Nobody, and nothing out of place. Everywhere, except the front door, was securely shut and fastened on the inside.

Then followed what she later looked back on as a small nightmare. She lifted the receiver and telephoned the old lady's doctor, then she returned upstairs to look for the letters between Miss Remington and the old lady's solicitor, for the firm's name had changed and at this moment Judy couldn't remember the new one. And that was when she discovered that all the correspondence was out of place. Either someone had been there or Miss Remington had herself hastily gone through it and left it so untidy, which wasn't likely. And the newer correspondence with the firm's new name and new telephone number was all missing.

She was so glad when the doctor came. She was shaking all over, and he could see that, as he asked her naturally why she hadn't telephoned him at once.

'I had the feeling that someone was in the house. I thought I saw a shadow at the top of the stairs. Besides, Miss Remington was so careful, she wouldn't fall. But of course,' she amended, thinking, 'she might have been too upset to be careful — her little dog is dead and she probably went downstairs to call someone . . . Well, she would have gone down to let the cats out,' she finished incoherently, 'because they aren't here.'

He looked at Judy very hard before speaking. 'Sit down,' he said. 'It's been a shock to you. Now ask yourself — the way you lock the place up when you leave, how do you suggest someone could have got in? Using the key?'

'Goodness, no. I had it in my bag. Why do you say that?'

'I had to make you see that you are raising needless problems,' he said. 'You may not know it, of course, but I have been treating Miss Remington for a heart condition for some time. She was rather vain and didn't like people to know she was ill or had to take pills. Did you never see them?'

'No, but she used to send me out of the room sometimes, suddenly, to get things.' She held her breath, wondering if he was not going to believe her.

The doctor apparently saw no problem. The old lady had no bruises on her body. 'I would have said she had got down the stairs, and just fell with a heart attack near the front door, letting the cats out possibly.'

Judy was only too glad to agree with him. The doctor, who knew the solicitor, telephoned him, and it should have all been smooth from then on. He had no thought of foul play; to him it was a heart attack, which was what he had been expecting. The solicitor and his clerk came over, Judy was paid the money that was due to her, and suddenly, on the eve of that tremendous clearing out job she was to have embarked on with Miss Remington, Judy's life in that house came to a sharp and clear ending.

The solicitor knew that the niece (who now superseded the birds' society in the Will) was out of the country. She was a wanderer, it appeared. There was going to be a long hunt for Miss Frances Banford, beginning with the only address they had, when she had first left England. He and his clerk took everything over in such a cool and efficient manner that Judy felt she was actually being shuffled out of the house. She forgot to mention that there was some correspondence missing; she forgot to mention the drawer in the base of the Buddha and the necklace, although when she thought about it she was sure the solicitor must know about that. All she could do was to surrender her front door key to the solicitor and go. Life must take a different twist for her now. She had to look for a new job.

Her doorkey had been in her pocket. She didn't look in her handbag until she reached her boarding-house, and then she saw the envelope containing the documents Noel had wanted her to show Miss Remington.

She sat on her bed and shivered. Now she would have to tell Noel and he would be so angry in his disappointment. The grey, cold day outside seemed to echo her unhappy thoughts. How awful to be like Miss Remington, and to die like that, so quickly, before you have done all the things you wanted to. Who would attend the funeral? The solicitor was arranging it all. She supposed he and the doctor would go.

She would have liked to suggest going herself, but — quite unwittingly, probably — they made her feel that she had no part in anything there any more. It would have been an intrusion on her part. She sighed and got up to enquire where Noel was, and when he was expected back.

Mrs. Venny didn't know, so Judy put her coat on again and prepared to start her round of the employment agencies, searching for some new job, preferably not with some old lady. The documents in her bag scared her without her knowing quite why, and the memory of the first old lady's death still weighed heavily on her. It was as she was walking down the street to the bus stop that she recalled the Buddha and the necklace in it, and she decided that she must telephone the solicitors about it. The doctor would know how to contact them. She waited till lunch-time, to be sure of his being back in his house, but he had been called out again on a confinement case and they didn't know when he'd be back.

Why should the Buddha nag at her like this, she asked herself. It was a secret lock. She hadn't known how to work it. Why should anyone else suspect there was something there? But a clever thief, she thought in sudden panic, could probably force the drawer or even smash the Buddha. It was all her fault. She should have remembered to tell them. She shouldn't have been intimidated like that. It was the speed with which they arrived at the house. Miss Remington's remains being whisked out of sight so quickly, and the need to close the house until the niece could be contacted. To them, Judy thought resentfully, it was just a small case, an unimportant old lady, a very unimportant death. It wouldn't even merit an inquest because the doctor had expected it. He had been in constant attendance. The doctor had said he would take the birds to his home. His housekeeper would look after them. But again, they had given no thought to the cats. Those poor old cats. They might be wandering about, waiting to be let in and fed and the neighbours wouldn't be kind to them. They hadn't liked them. But what could she do? She had no key now.

Her feet took her towards No. 17 Highview Avenue just the same. Nobody would do anything about the cats if she didn't. She might make a push to persuade a catless neighbour to oblige for the moment. She boarded a bus to save time, and scrabbled in her bag for some coppers that were usually loose in the bottom to pay her fare. Then her blood ran cold. She sat staring into her bag, oblivious of the conductor impatiently asking for her fare. At last, absently she gave it to him and took the ticket unseeingly. Her heart was madly racing. There, in the bottom of her handbag, lay a key. A brand-new freshly cut replica of the old lady's door key that she had herself surrendered to the solicitor's clerk hours before. She couldn't believe it. There was no doubt about it. Brand-new, but that key to Miss Remington's front door.

How had it got there?

She forced herself to remember the scene. The solicitor had come in person to see his old friend for the last time. Miss Remington had been his generation. Under his cool correct manner he had been shocked. The doctor had been telling him sharply that she wasn't the tough old bird she liked to pretend she was, and he had been absently playing with Judy's key, a worn, metal one, pitted with use. So where had this new one come from, and how had it got into her bag? It baffled her completely, and she fought to still the rising panic. She gave it up for the moment with the realisation that now she could get into the house, but panic returned with the thought that she would have to explain how she had acquired this new key. Absently she let herself in at the front door, only half aware that the postman, with a parcel for next door, was staring at her in some surprise. The old cats followed her in. They had been waiting below the steps. What had happened about the food in the larder for them? The milk? Curtains moved as the neighbours watched her. What an idiot, she should have bought some milk and openly brought it back with her, a legitimate excuse for being there. Already looking for excuses, she thought in dismay. But something had to be done about the animals, and she must go into the house now she had come so far.

And then, at the same place on the stairs, she felt the draught again.

The cats felt it, too, and froze by her heels. Someone was in the house again. She forced herself to go on up the stairs. All the doors were closed, but this time the draught didn't stop. It went on and on. She kept on up the stairs, and the draught got colder as she went, until she looked up at the ceiling. The trapdoor to the attic was open.

★　★　★

The animals pushed hard against her legs, shivering. I'm a coward, she told herself contemptuously, but she couldn't do anything about that. The cats decided her next movement. With their hair standing up, they squawked and shot down the stairs, and pushing against the door that had looked closed, they went in.

She felt the prickling of a new fear all down the back of her neck. She had carefully shut every door in the place. But she had gone, leaving the doctor, the solicitor and his clerk here. Had they left it ajar? She had to go and investigate. Pushing the door open further, she found it was the room in which the Eastern souvenirs were, and the Buddha containing the necklace.

She must see if it was still there. She forced her reluctant legs across to the window and pulled back the curtain to let in some light. Now she could see everything in the room, and that things had been moved about. By the lawyer's clerk, in taking his inventory, or by an interloper? But the clerk would not be likely to have left behind a very large and businesslike torch . . .

It was in the light of this torch that she saw the drawer under the Buddha had been forced. She pulled it out, and saw with a gusty sigh of relief that a diamond necklace still lay on the bed of velvet.

She hooked her finger under it and lifted it, as Miss Remington had done, but it didn't seem to be the same. Yet it looked the same pattern, the same arrangement of stones, of droplets, of the oval pendant hanging at its base. Yet the workmanship didn't seem so fine. Into her mind leapt the thought that it was merely a copy. Someone, she was convinced, had forced the drawer, taken the original and left this paste copy behind. She dropped it back into the drawer and pushed it shut.

Almost without thinking about it, she pulled the curtains across the window as she had found them, and still holding the big powerful torch, she left the room, the cowering cats against her legs. Then they started to purr, suggestively. They wanted food, something to drink. She was not their enemy; they remembered her. The kitchen, their throats purred, insistently. Let's go down to the kitchen.

She went down, glad to leave that open trapdoor behind her. But after she had found a little of yesterday's milk in the fridge, and settled the cats round two saucers, the sight of a long light alloy ladder reminded her. She took it up the stairs with her, and forced herself to climb up until she could see by the light of the torch, the whole of the attic. Nothing in the world would have persuaded her shaking limbs to climb into the attic, yet she felt she must see for herself if anyone was still there, although everything screamed out that whoever had been up there, must have crept down the stairs and left, while she had been doing her idiotic searching of all the rooms.

And then she found the answer to a question that had puzzled her since Miss Remington had insisted, only the day before, that someone kept getting into the house and moving things, stealing things. The questing beam of the torch found a hole in the brick wall dividing the attic from its neighbour in the next house. The intruder had got in from next door, easily, laughing at her careful locking of doors, windows, shutters. What did bolts and bars mean to him? But how had he got down and returned to the attic without using this light step ladder? There was nothing so convenient as a let-down loft ladder in this house. She directed the beam of light downwards. Marks in the dust of the attic floor suggested a way. The intruder must have brought his own rope ladder, pulling it up after him . . .

Judy felt ill. Ill to think of how vulnerable poor Miss Remington had been, in a terrace of houses where presumably the attics all connected with a hole large enough for a man to crawl through. How to tell which house he had come from would be impossible. She thought of the shadow she had seen, which must have been the intruder. Her own spontaneous first thought had been that it had seemed like Noel . . . But all this didn't explain that new front door key that she had found in her handbag, she thought, as she returned to the reassuring warmth of the kitchen. Unless the intruder had been in the house long enough to slip it in her bag while she was looking for the telephone number of the solicitors. Yes, that could have happened. She had left her bag on the hall table.

Her scalp prickled. She knew she must contact the solicitors and tell them these things, *somehow*. She had shut the trapdoor but for all the good it had done, she might as well have left it open. In any case, she must provide for the cats, although the birds had already been removed. She had heard the doctor say his housekeeper would look after them. But Judy still couldn't remember the new name of the solicitors nor their new address. It just eluded her. So the thought of looking up a telephone book for them was useless. And while she was racking her brains to know what to do, the telephone began to ring.

Strange, how sinister it sounded in that silent house. She stood there rooted to the spot. Who would ring at this time of the day? Although she made no move to answer it, it didn't stop, as if the caller knew someone was there. It went on and on and on ringing, until at last in desperation she picked up the receiver.

'I know you're there in the house,' a muffled voice said. 'Don't be clever and tell anyone about the attic trapdoor or the Buddha, or I might feel I must tell someone about how you unlocked that front door and got into the house after you had surrendered your own key.'

'Who's there? Who are you?' Judy asked desperately. 'Where are you? How do you know these things?' But of course, no answer came. The receiver at the other end was quietly replaced, and only the ringing tone was now there, to mock her.

She fumbled putting the receiver

down, and almost dropped it. She was shaking all over with the realisation that whoever had been speaking, must have been the intruder. He must have been in the house somewhere, while the doctor and solicitor were there, and heard her say she had no other key. He must have watched Miss Remington's body being removed from the hall; coldly, callously, robbed the dead of that diamond necklace, put a fake one in its place, and now was willing to threaten Judy into silence about those things.

She must leave this house at once. But the cats? She couldn't leave them shut in there. She hadn't got it in her to turn them out, either. Neighbours? She knew without a second thought, that that would be futile. Hadn't Miss Remington complained often enough about her neighbours never helping anyone, and hating her cats? There was only one thing she could do; telephone a message to the doctor. He would do something, if only to call up the solicitors to go back to the house. She lifted the receiver again, but the line was dead.

That was the final shock. Someone had cut the outside wire, so that she couldn't telephone anyone. But she could go to a callbox or . . . did that mean she wouldn't be allowed to get out of the house?

★   ★   ★

A long time afterwards she let herself out of the back door and stood thinking. The garden was small, a pocket-handkerchief sized lawn with a narrow flower bed round it, and a lane down which the dustmen came to collect the rubbish.

Next door someone was hanging out washing and a head poked enquiringly over the wall. The hard face of the cleaning woman, inquisitive as always. The two elderly bachelors who lived there were never seen, but the woman who cleaned and washed for them was one who had a lot to say about the cats and the old dog.

She said now, 'Oh, it's you. Thought I saw you come back. Having a poke around, are you? Don't let the solicitor catch you, that's all.'

'I was worried about the cats, but they've come back now,' Judy said. 'I don't know what to do about them.' She didn't like the woman but it was curiously comforting to have someone, anyone, to speak to, after the nightmare in that house. 'I suppose I shall have to go to the police with them.'

The woman sniffed. 'Some people have got a nerve! Fancy you thinking about going to the police!' and she started to laugh.

'What's wrong with that? People go and ask them for advice. They'd tell me of a vet or a cat's home, I suppose.'

'Well, talk's cheap. But you won't go near a policeman, not you, my girl. Not with the company you keep!'

Judy asked angrily, 'What's that supposed to mean?'

'Oh, nothing, just that boy-friend of

yours. I bet he won't thank you to go near any police, nor you won't want to neither. Just scratching around, hoping someone'll offer to take 'em in, aren't you? Well, don't look at me. Nor anyone else. Who'd want them smelly old cats about the place?'

Judy said, half to herself, 'Then I'll have to take them somewhere to be put down. I can't leave them here, to starve.'

'How will you take 'em?' the woman asked.

'There's a cat basket,' Judy remembered, and went inside again. She stood listening. Again the house felt it wasn't empty. Why hadn't she told that woman she had been threatened on the telephone, before the line had gone dead? But that woman was as hostile in her way as the unknown man who had called her up, with his soft muffled voice, as if speaking through a scarf.

Blind terror took hold of Judy. The cat basket was in the bottom of the kitchen dresser. She bundled the cats in it, locked the back door and ran softly down the path to the door to the lane. But on opening it, she saw a man poking about in a sack. He looked at her, and went on with his poking. She went back into the garden again. Who was he? Someone's odd job man or . . . someone watching her? Her terror was communicating itself to the animals, who moved restlessly. She hurried back to the house, unlocked the door and went in, locking it behind her. Now she must go out the front way. But in the street a man in a short waterproof with a zip front was leaning against Noel's lamp-post, doing nothing in particular; on the other side of the road a man was comparing house numbers with a paper in his hand. Innocent or . . . there to stop her movements?

But the milkman's van was also out there, and while he was delivering, she told herself feverishly, nobody would molest her. She hurried up the street. As she ran, her mind caught on to the memory of the street where the solicitor's office was. Their name still eluded her but she remembered the office. She took the cats there.

Her relief at having found them was so great that she hysterically called to mind their new names. Now she could remember it, now it didn't matter.

The solicitor happened to be passing through the outer office at the time and stopped short at the sight of her. 'Good heavens, girl, you look as if you'd seen a ghost. What have you got there?'

She had found him. Now she could tell the solicitor everything. But her voice wouldn't work. At last, she managed to say, 'I found the cats, but I don't know what to do with them.'

'Oh, well, put them down there. Miss Jones will — ah — arrange something.' Now he was annoyed with himself for having been caught. Another minute and he could have slipped into his office and missed her. She looked as if she might be going to be tiresome. 'Now do go and get some food or a cup of tea or something,' he said quickly.

'You mustn't worry! Everything is in our hands now. All you have to do is to get yourself another job and forget about poor Miss Remington. You did your best and she told me herself she was pleased with you,' and he gave her the sort of shoulder pat that was also a small push. He had an urgent phone call to make.

'Yes, but I have something to tell you,' Judy gasped, but he'd vanished into his own sanctum. The moment had passed.

The elderly secretary, already taking charge of the cat basket, said, 'If you've thought of something, it's all right. Tell me. Don't worry Mr. Wardlaw.' She got her shorthand notebook, and held her pencil poised about it.

Judy thought what it would sound like, if she said, 'I meant to mention that there was a diamond necklace worth thousands, hidden in a secret drawer of a little Buddha only it's been stolen, replaced by what I think is a fake one, by a thief who lets himself in through the attics and he put a duplicate front door key in my handbag when I wasn't looking, and he later threatened me on the telephone, before cutting the phone wires.' The office boy was standing staring at her, too, ready to be entertained by any revelations this scared-looking girl might make. Judy dried up. She shook her head, muttered vague thanks, and hurried out. But she must tell someone. The police? She was passing a police station at that moment. Two policemen outside exchanged a joke and a brief laugh. In her over-wrought state she was sure she would further their gaiety by her very incredible story. She turned away, and as she did so, she caught sight of the man in the zippered jacket who had been leaning against the lamp-post in Highview Avenue. Was he following her?

Judy panicked. She fought down the shocking coincidence that he should be there by accident and not interested in her movements. Mrs. Venny's — she would go there. That man would have no reason to be there, so if he were still in sight he must surely be following her.

She had an overwhelming desire to be in her own room at the boarding-house. She would be safe there, she told herself. And while there, she must remove the documents from her handbag and return them to Noel's room; she could push the envelope containing them under his door. She felt better with that decision and weaved her way through the stalls in the market, stopping to buy some rolls filled with ham and tomato, at the coffee stall at one end. She had had no breakfast, she recalled. No wonder she felt empty and queer! No wonder she imagined she was being followed! She brightened, and bought an apple and a banana at a fruit stall, and on second thoughts she returned to the coffee stall and sat on a high stool with hot sweet tea she ordered. Sipping it, she began to feel much better, until she caught sight again of that man in the zippered jacket, at the next stall, examining a little clock.

The coffee stall man said, 'What's the matter gel? Seen an accident or something?' There was genuine concern in his voice. She looked terrible.

She dragged her glance from the man in the jacket. She wished she could tell the coffee stall man all about it. He looked a fatherly type. But the man looking at the clock would hear her. She shook her head, and finished her tea. People milling round the stall cloaked her retreat and she left the market and got to Mrs. Venny's boarding-house without a sight of the man. She was shaking again by the time she reached her own room. She went straight to the window, keeping well back to peer from behind the curtains. But the street was empty.

She sat on the bed, limp with relief. Now she could eat her food and feel better. But in her haste to leave the coffee stall, at the sight of that man, she had lost her food. She remembered she had left it on the counter.

She felt like weeping. A revulsion for

what she must do — emerging from that house to search for a new job — swept over her. She wanted to leave the place behind. Start afresh in some completely new place where she hadn't been filled with fears, as in this town. Where could she go? London — yes, London! She had heard someone say once that the only place you could hide in successfully was a big city like London. But to do that, she must go to a Post Office and draw out her savings.

Mrs. Venny opened the door and came in carrying a pile of fresh sheets, and at the sight of Judy she pulled up short. 'Oh, it's you! What are *you* doing at this time of the day? Why aren't you at work? Took ill, were you? You *do* look queer, come to think of it. But I can't have illness in my house. Bad for the other boarders. Flu's about, they say. Right down catching. Better look in at the doctor's, hadn't you, before his surgery closes? That was why you couldn't take any food this morning, I reckon. Sickening for something, you were.'

Judy nodded, dragged on her coat again and went out. It was easier to go than to argue. Perhaps she had got something coming on; a chill, or perhaps she was suffering from delayed shock. She should have told Mrs. Venny that she was afraid of a man following her. No, that wouldn't do. Mrs. Venny had a pathological fear of things 'looking peculiar', and 'calling in the police', a thing which she always said was 'so bad for an address'. As if the police were some sort of menace, and not the helpful bunch of people that small children are taught to go to, when they are lost.

Where was she going, Judy asked herself? If she was to go to London she should be packing her things, stripping down that little room of the few personal things she possessed, dragging down the big old case from the top of the wardrobe. She wilted at the thought of so much effort. What would Mrs. Venny say? She would want a month's rent in lieu of notice, too. Mrs. Venny was much against her 'guests' leaving in an unseemly hurry. That, too, was bad for the house, she always said. Trapped, Judy walked unseeingly. The man in the zippered jacket followed her with ease. She neither looked round nor up nor down the street but plodded on like a sleep-walker.

When she reached the railway station she stopped as if in surprise. She must have been thinking about this all the time. She went up to the ticket clerk and asked what the price of a single to London was. It happened to be the exact amount that she had in her purse, and that was supposed to last her until the following week, when she should have been paid. Only now she had no job. She nodded and walked away, to stand in the middle of the booking hall, thinking. If she got to London, what would she do for a roof over her head, without luggage, without a job? By the same token, what would she do in this town, with a man who was following her, and the memory of No. 17 Highview Avenue?

She walked to the train times board and looked as if she were studying it, while she thought. Something was so wrong about all this. It struck her then that the biggest reason for her running away was that she didn't want to see Noel again. That was the first time she had ever admitted it to herself even. Now her heart started racing as she thought of him, and when she had started to be like this. First Miss Remington saying she didn't trust him, then the cleaning woman next door making remarks about him, and these two opinions adding themselves to all her recent fears where he was concerned. But, her mind queried he was all she had, wasn't he? Why hadn't she waited for him to return, told him all about what had happened? Because she was afraid of him. It was as simple as that. Afraid to admit to him that Miss Remington, the rich woman he had wanted so badly to sign those documents, was now dead. Whatever he had wanted of Miss Remington, she was gone, and all her possessions held for a person who was a suddenly remembered niece, someone who had money of her own, surely, since she travelled all over the world, instead of going to a job in the town?

Judy turned and made up her mind. A single ticket to London, before that man could find her again. She visibly jumped when someone put a hand on her arm but it was only a porter, broom in one hand, and a note in the other, which he held out for her. 'Gent pointed you out, miss, and said to give you this. Urgent, he said it was,' and he waited, so she found a coin, which he looked contemptuously at, as he took it and then shuffled away. She was almost too afraid to open the note, but it had to be opened, and it was from Noel. TELEPHONE ME AT THIS NUMBER, ONE OF THE CALL BOXES ON THE STATION, he had written with a peremptory tone that he used sometimes when he wasn't pleased with her.

There was a line of call boxes, half of

them empty at this time of the day. She went into one and called the number and Noel answered as if he had been by the telephone, waiting. So quick that she paused to wonder where he could have been to give the porter the note for her. 'Noel, where are you?' she cried.

'Never mind that, love. Something's come up and you're the only one I can ask to help me out. Will you do something for me?'

It took her so much by surprise that she forgot to tell him of the things that had happened to her. She could only wonder why he had his 'kind' voice on, and called her 'love' again. So she said, 'If I can,' in a bewildered voice.

'It's important, love, and you're the only one who can help me. I have a very important packet I must get delivered to London. Will you take it for me?'

'Yes, but how did you know I'd be free to go?' she asked, suspicious now. But Mrs. Venny knew she wasn't at work. 'Oh, you've been back to the house. Did Mrs. Venny tell you I'd gone home from work?'

Somehow she couldn't bear to mention Miss Remington to him, and the impatient note was back in his voice again. 'Judy, never mind questions. Listen. The London train is in the station now. Yes, yes, I did get it from Mrs. Venny that you weren't at work. That's why I'm asking you to do this. Now scoot, like a good girl, and get your ticket. You've only got to pick it up. It is paid for. Buck up or you'll lose that train!'

'But the packet I've got to deliver. You haven't told me where — '

'It's with the ticket,' he snapped, his patience quite deserting him. That was more like Noel, so she jumped to it, hastily replacing the receiver, and picked up her handbag and rushed over to the ticket clerk where she had so recently been asking about the price of a ticket. He saw her coming and held out the small package and the ticket, and even told her on which platform the train was standing. Like Noel, he urged her to hurry.

She had to run. A man held open a door and she was helped up into the train. The door slammed behind her. She was on a train going to London . . .

As the train moved out of the station, Judy staggered through the open doorway into the almost empty compartment. Double seats with high backs, two to a table, stretched before her. She flopped into the first seat and closed her eyes and waited until she had controlled her rapid breathing and her fiercely beating heart. She opened them at last, and pushed her hair back. The tops of one or two heads were to be seen above the seat backs, but for the most part the compartment was almost empty and blessedly peaceful. Now she must try to clear her head, think. But she couldn't. Light-headed, through lack of food, shock, fear, and all the things that had happened to her already that day.

She must have dozed a little. The

train's pulling up at one of those un-explained stops and the sharp silence, punctuated by a hissing sound, made her open her eyes. The train crept along slowly, jerking and stopping, until another train passed, and then it picked up speed again. But she felt better now. She could remember the ticket she was still auto-matically clutching and examine it. It was a single ticket. She stared at it, puzzled. A single ticket? Didn't Noel expect her to come back, then? But of course, he probably only had the bare cash for the one way journey. Last night he had been so short of funds that he had let her buy her own meal, so it was hardly likely that he was in a position to buy a return ticket for her.

She sighed and put it in her purse. The packet, the reason for the journey, lay on the table in front of her. She turned it over and read the address. It was addressed in thick black ink and block capitals, to a Mr. Rosenberg at a number in Hatton Garden, London. Hatton Garden? Judy stared at it and felt the colour drain from her face, as she recalled the only thing that Hatton Garden was famous for.

3

In the days and weeks that followed, Judy often looked back on that train journey and tried to think, to picture the scattering of people in the compartment picked up at the first stop, and to remember if anyone at any time had looked at her or the young woman who had drifted in at some point and sat on the other side of the table, to stare fixedly out of the window, acute anxiety all over her face. But try as Judy would, she could remember nobody clearly, only the girl on the other side of her table. It was a sparsely occupied compartment of middle of the day people, who were supremely unconcerned with their fellow travellers, and their faces remained obstinately blank.

Of course, the shock of Miss Remington's death had taken its toll, coupled with the fears that had built up by Noel's pressure and general attitude, and the conviction that she had been followed by the man in the zippered jacket. On top of all that, she had had little or nothing to eat, and most of the time she had felt frankly lightheaded. She remembered dozing off sometimes, dreaming horrifying dreams about the packet she was to deliver for Noel. Although she had stowed it away in her bag, she felt that everyone around her knew it was there. And at all times there was the feeling, awake or dreaming, that she was surrounded by enemies.

During the times she dozed, the movement of other people half disturbed her. The voice calling out the times of lunch as he went through, and the constant rumble of the door beside her as it was slid first one way then another, to permit people to come in or go out. Once the train swerved round a corner as the attendant passed with a tray of coffee and Judy heard the splash of liquid on the floor. The girl sitting facing her had sharply ejaculated as some of the hot coffee had gone on to her hand, but Judy didn't catch what she said. She opened her eyes enquiringly and the girl muttered, 'I don't like train journeys,' and scrubbed her hand dry with a handkerchief.

Judy felt something should be said to that, so she admitted that she didn't care for them either. The girl asked her where she was going and when Judy said London, the girl muttered, 'Lucky you. I'm going to Pillerwick.'

Pillerwick. Where was Pillerwick? Well, it sounded like Pillerwick. The girl had an odd accent, perhaps an impediment in her speech. Judy had to make the effort to listen, and somehow that was taken as encouragement and the girl began to talk.

'I've got to talk to someone,' she muttered. 'I'm so worried. I'm off my head with worry. I don't know what to do!'

Judy sat up. She had the sort of face that invited confidence and it was not in her nature to refuse a cry for help.

The girl took it as permission to go on, and disclosed that she was a nurse, which explained her plain dark raincoat and schoolgirl felt hat. Her hair was tightly drawn back so that it wasn't possible to see what colour it was, and the most ordinary face in the world suffered under the brim of the hat. Its suffering was the thing Judy remembered afterwards; it blotted out the colour of eyes, the shape of mouth and eyebrows. It dominated everything. That, and the curious impediment in the speech.

The girl started talking and once having started, didn't seem to be able to stop. Getting it all off her chest, Judy thought. But it was so difficult to understand half she said, because she talked at a great rate as if afraid she wouldn't be able to tell it all in the time at her disposal. Judy missed a lot of it because of people going through, and the door being slid back and forth beside her, and the girl lowered her voice dramatically whenever anyone came near, but Judy did gather enough from the involved narrative to gain the impression that like herself, the girl was being persecuted. She showed Judy a letter which had arrived that morning and was worrying her. It was, she said, from someone called Vonette Quorn (or so it sounded like) who lived at 7a Challeybourn Street, Pillerwick. If she hadn't told Judy all that, Judy would never have gleaned it from the handwriting of the letter which was almost indecipherable. The difficulties mounted because the more excited the nurse grew about her troubles, the more pronounced the impediment in her speech became, which made it difficult for Judy to understand, and the more Judy asked for amplification of this or that detail, the more emotional the nurse grew, which slurred her speech more, and she seemed to have difficulty in stopping herself from bursting into tears.

Yet in an odd way the recital of someone else's troubles seemed to alleviate her own, or at least to take her mind off them. For the moment Judy appeared to have shaken off the man she thought was following her, and now, at this distance, she began to wonder whether that man had been interested in her at all. The nurse's story swamped her own. She had been on a private case, she said. The person called Vonette Quorn had written a vaguely threatening letter. Judy couldn't determine whether there was reason for it or whether the nurse was protecting someone. Then all of a sudden the nurse leaned forward and said, more distinctly than she had uttered so far, 'What would you say if I told you that they're trying to kill me? They're going to kill me? Perhaps today!'

'But you must go to the police, if that's true,' Judy said, and then she thought of her own case and the hundred reasons why she herself wouldn't have taken such a step. The nurse shook her head fiercely. 'No, I dare not. There are *reasons*. That's what people always say — why don't you go the police? But have you ever been to them? They don't care. You get taken to the desk sergeant and he takes down your name and address and wants facts. Who's got facts? What would you tell him, if you were me? How would you tell him all I've been telling you?' and terror was in her eyes and in the grip of her hand on Judy's.

Judy's heart started to hammer again and all her own fears rushed back. It was true. If you had an unbelievable story, you couldn't expect help, yet your own hideous nightmare you lived in was nonetheless real.

The nurse said, 'I want to ask you something. I have to go to the loo — I'm scared stiff they'll get me. You come with me. They won't touch me if there are two of us. Please!'

'But *who* will get you?' Judy felt impelled to ask.

The nurse said a name but she turned her head sharply to look at a man who was going by as she said it, so Judy didn't hear distinctly. The nurse said, 'Let's go, while it's quiet. Must go now — the train will soon be pulling into a station. Come on.'

Judy got up with her. It might be more sense, come to think of it, if they both went along the swaying train. She had been thinking of doing that journey herself. Now they had to entangle with the sliding door, which was hard to push, and people were going through. Outside the compartment was the lobby where the train's door was. Several men, suitcases round their feet, were already stationed there, ready to jump out when the train stopped. The nurse seemed to hesitate, looking at them.

Judy said, 'Come on, it isn't in this one. We'll have to go through the next compartment,' but the nurse turned and wrestled with the door.

Then it became confused. A man was coming out, which made the nurse back, and Judy was pushed away. Suddenly the men were all round the nurse, and she uttered a choking scream, as if someone's hand was over her mouth. Judy couldn't see her, and pulled at the men all round her. Her cry had been obliterated in the rumble of that door behind them being closed. And then the struggle resolved itself into something quite horrific. Judy was held back by the man behind her, while, before her eyes, the window in the train door was dropped and a dark shape was pushed through, a wailing cry intermingling with the scream of the train's warning whistle. They had thrown the nurse out of the train!

Judy's voice suddenly became unleashed. She heard herself shout, 'You've killed her!' and struggling, she got free of them and without thinking, her hand shot up and pulled the communication cord. The great train shuddered and began its braking process.

It had been a reflex action of utter horror on her part. She had never before pulled a communication cord, never before been on a train on which someone else had pulled it. She had no idea of the jerking back, the cries of other passengers, the confusion, the myriad cries asking what happened, nor the way she herself was thrown against the door, hit her head and slithered to the ground. Utter confusion reigned and when she did gather her wits to get to her feet, the train had stopped, a new set of people were around her including the guard who not unnaturally wanted to know why his train had been stopped.

Not once, but a hundred times, it seemed to Judy, looking back over the weeks, and answering a hundred different people who closely questioned her about that day on the train, did she try to recall what precisely happened then. It was all such a muddle. Walking, no, half-running, along the track, looking for a body she swore she had seen thrown out of that open window, and finding nothing. Asking, frenziedly asking other passengers, if they hadn't heard that terrible cry as the nurse had been thrown out, but nobody had heard such a cry, only a wail from the train's own warning system that it was approaching the next stop. Asking, asking, hundreds of people, it seemed, but no one, not a single person, had seen or heard anything of the things that Judy told the guard had led to her stopping the train. In fact, she couldn't find anyone who remembered seeing her talking to a nurse. But, then, nobody seemed to remember seeing Judy sitting there at that table just inside the door.

Judy's voice grew higher and higher, and she wasn't surprised when it was said firmly by someone (who, the guard? Someone in authority) that she should be taken to the station master's office and a doctor sent for.

'But I have to go to London! I have an urgent mission — I must deliver this packet!' she cried, scrabbling in her handbag for it.

There was no packet in her handbag addressed to the man in Hatton Garden.

To her life's end, she thought, she would never forget the awful sensation when she found the package had gone. 'Those men must have taken it — they must have robbed me, yes, that's it! — when we were struggling, just before they threw the nurse out of the window!' she heard herself say, her voice rising. And to her life's end, she thought, she would never forget the looks on the faces ringed around her; not exactly smiling, not exactly pitying, nor even looking as if they were thinking, 'I told you so'; but a combination of all these things, which made her feel uncertain in her own mind that those things had happened.

'But this is ridiculous!' she shouted. 'It is true, what I'm saying! The nurse had a suitcase — I'll find it for you. It was under the table — I kept catching my feet against it,' and she pushed through the crowds to her seat and looked underneath. There was no suitcase there.

There was a roaring in her ears. She kept seeing Miss Remington on the hall floor, dead; the little dog dead; the cats terrified of the open trapdoor. Noel and his pressing for those documents to be signed. The man in the zip jacket who had been following her. Her one-time employer who had fallen out of the window, and now this nurse. Noel had said she had a jinx and that people close to her had awful things happen to them. She put her hands over her ears as if to shut out the sound of the things that were being said in her head, and someone helped her into a seat. The train was moving again. Someone promised the guard he would stay with her until they pulled into the next station, and he sat down beside her, and a woman woman sat facing her, and they weren't going to move.

She slumped back in her seat and shut her eyes. Think, think, there must have been some movement near her, someone's hand in her bag taking that packet, and carefully closing the bag again? She would have to buy a new bag, she thought, in a frightened way. One with somewhere in it where she could keep things safely. A bag where nobody could take anything out, nor anyone put something in, such as that brand new key to the front door of No. 17.

The train pulled in to the station and

she was taken to the station master's office and sat down in front of a big coal fire, but even the heat of that didn't stop her shivering.

There was official telephoning going on. The guard was telling the station master what had happened. The station master said he was wondering what the heck was going on. A hospital was mentioned, and the police, and then someone said, 'Well, here's someone who might help. It's Dr. Marland, just a minute, I'll get him.' More people coming in, the guard going to the door. Telephoning, fussing about getting the train on its way. And then someone sat down by her and a pair of very kind brown eyes looked into hers, and said, 'How are you feeling now?'

She said, 'Terrible,' but her face felt stiff and she had a curious reluctance to speak. She wanted to be left alone, to wait until this deadening of her thinking processes lifted, and she could sort it all out for herself.

'Well, I think I know just what to do

about that. I'm Dr. Marland, by the way. They all know me here. Ask anyone. What I think would be a good idea would be to come back with me to the house. Surgery's closed now, but my mother is there and she'd love to give you a nice cup of tea. How would that be?'

He didn't speak soothingly to her as if she weren't all there, and he didn't sound hectoring, either. It was a nice in-between sort of voice. *Easy*, that was it. His whole manner and appearance was easy. He looked at someone over her shoulder and said, 'I know you're busy, Sergeant. How about leaving this to me for a while. I'll let you know how things are going.' And to Judy he said, half apologetically, 'We're in a bit of a mess in this town at the moment. There's been a bit of trouble at one of the factories. All the police are out. The hospital can't take any more. Explosion, you know,' as if it were the most natural thing in the world. He took Judy's arm and said, 'My car's outside. I've actually got one more visit to do and then the rounds are finished. Like to come?'

She thought, He *is* being soothing, but he's pretending everything's all right. Where will he take me? and panic surged through her.

She said, rather sharply, 'What I do doesn't matter. What are *they* going to do? About that nurse who was thrown out of the train window? She's lying along the track somewhere! Why don't they look for her?'

He said, 'They tell me the police are searching now. It'll be all right.' He smiled. 'Don't worry.'

He was very tall, rather broad, comfortable, just as one would expect a country doctor to look. Somehow his unflappable manner penetrated her shell of fear and she let him lead her out to his car. 'Let me know, won't you, if there are any further developments?' he said to the station master, who nodded.

His car was comfortable, too. Not too new, but very dearly looked after, and it ran so sweetly. He drove like a man who loved driving, and when Judy was settled in the seat by him, he gentled the car out of the station yard through a comfortable country town whose name she didn't know, and through residental roads to his patient's house.

She thought, will he lock me in? Will he trust me? The minute he goes I'll get out and telephone the police, to find out if they've found that nurse . . .

The doctor didn't get out of the car. He tooted gently on the horn and an old man straightened up from behind a bush in the front garden and came out to the car with a pleased smile, to receive from the doctor a long packet, carefully wrapped. 'They're a very good pair of secateurs,' the doctor smiled. 'I'd like you to have them. I've got another pair. And it'll please your wife.'

He drove on with a wave, the old man's thanks in their ears. He said conversationally to Judy, 'He'd be sitting moping by his wife's bedside if I didn't encourage him to keep that front garden going. She likes to sit in her chair and watch him, for an hour or two. Better than all the medicines.'

Judy nodded, not speaking. He had an insidious charm which she fought against. She didn't understand why he had taken her off the train with so little persuasion from anyone. She didn't understand what was happening at all. She should have stayed on that train and gone to London. But she had no luggage and she had lost the packet. This time last week she and Noel were going to be married, at least, so he kept saying. In just a week he had reduced her to a shivering wretch, afraid of those documents he wanted Miss Remington to sign; frightened sick because he had threatened to tell about the other old lady. And why had she been frightened? She didn't know. It was just, she supposed, because people were inclined to believe what things looked like, not what they really were.

The doctor turned into the drive of a pleasant house, in a road that terminated in a main road of shops. There was a lamp hanging over the gate arch with a big capital 'D' on it for doctor, and there was a supercilious cat on one of the gate posts, pretending it didn't know the man who was slowly and carefully driving the car into the garage.

'This is my house and here comes my mother, and if you take my advice you will accept any invitation she throws out for you to stay the night. She likes having young people to stay.'

'Why should she? She doesn't know me!' Judy whispered.

'She misses my sister, who's got married and gone too far away to live,' he said, and made everything seem quite normal.

He took Judy in and explained briefly to the smart, trim woman with iron grey hair nicely cut and waved, 'Mother, this young lady has had a rather odd experience on the train, and I thought if we let her get over it a bit, she'd be better here than at the hospital. Okay with you?'

She said, 'Of course. Come in, my dear. You do look poorly,' and like her son, her easy manner enfolded Judy into the household. She had a light lunch and felt a lot better, and then it was time for some explanations.

But the telephone rang, and the doctor's mother went out to answer it. Her guarded replies finally got the doctor up on his feet. He excused himself to Judy and went out to the hall, closing the door behind him. His replies were guarded to whoever was calling, too.

Judy got up and went to the door. She couldn't help herself. They were talking about her. She heard his mother say to the doctor, 'What's this about a body they can't find? Is that nice girl connected with this?' and he said, in a not very pleased voice, 'I think she might be.'

'Well, why didn't the police handle it. Why did you bring her here, David?'

He said, 'They're a bit thrown out of their stride this morning with the trouble at Bryant's factory, and now this train business. Sergeant Neville said to me, 'For the love of heaven take this girl home and try to get something out of her — in any case I think it's more up your street than ours'.'

'What did he mean by that?'

'A little matter of someone being thrown from a train but no body to be found, mother. Let's have a little talk with her.'

Judy rushed back to her chair and just managed to be sitting there with the cat standing on tiptoe staring at her, when he came in. Ignoring the doctor the cat satisfied herself that she approved of Judy, and calmly climbed up to her lap, thought a bit, then suddenly curled into a ball and went to sleep.

'Well, young lady, my cat doesn't often show such approval of a person and I trust her judgment.'

'But Sergeant Neville wouldn't be unduly influenced,' Judy retorted.

He pulled a face. 'If they'd found the person you said you saw thrown from the train, they'd have let you resume your journey. To London, I think it was.'

She nodded.

'As it is, they tell me there is no body

anywhere, and no evidence of any body having been there. They searched a long way back up the track. Care to tell me something about what happened?'

'Why? Why do you care one way or the other? Why did they give me into your care? I would have thought the police would question me. After all, I was robbed on the train, but they didn't believe a word I said.'

'Perhaps because when a communication cord is pulled they like to be shown some reason for it. Nobody on the train saw the nurse you said you were talking to. Nobody noticed any scuffle or heard the scream you mentioned. And there was no case under the table. Nothing to show she'd ever been there.'

'You don't believe me either!'

'I haven't heard the story. I've only been told with rather stark brevity by my old friend the police sergeant, the story the way he heard it. I'm ready to hear your side, in detail, if you like.'

It was so nice in his mother's sitting-room. So *safe*, she found herself thinking.

His mother was nice, and so was he, but their conversation in the hall showed they were realists. So what was his interest? Judy asked him bluntly. 'I suppose you think I'm not quite responsible for my actions, and that is a thing you are personally interested in. Is that it?'

'Would that be such a bad thing?' he asked her.

It wasn't the answer she expected. 'What would happen to me if I didn't tell you?'

'Probably no more than a fine for pulling the communication cord without reason,' he said coolly. 'People do these things. They make up dramatic stories to account for their actions. I will say this,' he said in an altered voice. 'It is not usually a young and pretty girl, but an older person, one who has been lonely, or suffered, or feels resentful. I don't think any of those things apply to you. Tell me about the person you think you saw thrown out of the train window.'

'I didn't think I saw it. I did see it.

After all, she expected it, or some such attack on her. That was why I was with her,' Judy said bitterly. 'She *asked* me to go with her, because she was afraid someone would try to kill her. And I saw it, I saw it!' and in spite of herself, her voice rose again.

Now she had his complete attention. 'Let's start at the beginning. How come she was telling you all this?'

'She was so worried. She looked worried sick. We got talking by accident, when the attendant spilt some coffee on her hand. Then she said she'd got to tell someone what was troubling her.'

'And that was?' he asked, and began lighting a short briar pipe. Judy watched him. Strange how comfortable was the sight of a man in an armchair in front of a fire, a coal fire, with a cat purring, and pipe being lit.

'Oh, I don't know. It was a very involved story. There was a letter she'd had from someone.'

'Did you believe she'd had a letter?'

Judy shrugged. 'She showed it to me.

It was from someone called Vonette Quorn of 7a Challeybourn Street, Pillerwick. She told me what was in it because I couldn't read the writing.'

'But you remembered the name and address?'

'Well, that's what it sounded like. She'd got a sort of funny accent, like with a cleft roof, you know what I mean?'

He nodded and asked for this person to be described, but Judy could only tell him it was a plainish face, very worried, under a nurse's felt hat. 'She had a dark navy raincoat on. I remembered thinking what awful clothes to wear. And she was worried sick about this person writing to her.'

'Why?' he said, and casually wrote down the name and address.

'She thought the letter was threatening. I couldn't understand half of what she said. Why are you writing this down?'

He hesitated. 'Look, when someone says they've seen a murder — well, you did say that, didn't you? — then it has to be investigated, especially when a long-distance train has been stopped the way you did it today. I suppose you don't want to alter your statement? You don't think after all that some people were larking about with that nurse?'

She stared at him, and the way she slowly shook her head, remembering that tortured face and the sick insistance that she accompany a complete stranger to the loo because she feared for her life, convinced him.

'Yes, I thought you were sure of your facts. So now you've given me someone's name, I can give it to the sergeant to verify. That should give us a start. Don't look like that at me. The state you were in this morning, I did think it was better for me to talk to you here than for you to be taken to the station for questioning. They had enough on their plate already, so you might have been there waiting for a long time.'

'Well, if you want more facts, I can give you the nurse's name,' Judy said unexpectedly, still a little dazed with the thought that her actions in stopping the train and reporting the death of the nurse, should merit her being taken to the police station.

'You knew it? I thought you said you didn't know her.'

'I didn't. But you see, something happened to me early this morning . . . I had a shock, and I haven't been able to think clearly since. I've just remembered what she said her name was. Lemira Jeacock.'

The way he looked at her didn't seem odd. Judy wondered how she could have brought herself to utter that name. It was too ridiculous. What sort of name was it, anyway? Not foreign, just peculiar, no . . . just very, very unusual.

The doctor wrote it down. 'So she was in a state about this threatening letter. Did she say who this Vonette person was, in relation to her?'

Judy shook her head. 'Well, she might have. I didn't understand all she said.'

David said, 'Well, at least we have something to go on. I'll let my old friend the sergeant have these to mull over. I think I'll have a chat with him now, as a matter of fact.'

He wasn't long on the telephone. He came back and said, 'I ought to have thought. He's gone off duty. But they've taken a note of these names, and they can be checking them.'

'How can they?' She was frightened, without quite knowing why.

David said, 'Well, they have their methods. I've worked with the police on cases in this town before. They're a good lot. Don't worry, it will be all right.'

He sat down again and looked at her. 'Now you, how came you to be on that train without luggage, and I haven't yet heard what you were robbed of. Did you tell the police that?'

Despair filled her as she tried to find words to frame what was by now to him an extremely involved story altogether. 'I was robbed of a packet that someone had asked me to deliver,' she said carefully. 'I've no idea what was in it.' And as she thought, his face changed. It

97

was too impossible for words.

'You'll have to do better than that, won't you?' he said, after a silence. 'Well, look at it this way. It must have been of either great value (sentimental or otherwise) to merit asking someone to make a long train journey to take it in person, and the least the sender could have done was to let you have some idea what it contained. Well, didn't you ask?'

'It was arranged in rather a rush,' she said helplessly.

'By whom? Who was this sender?'

'A man called Noel Ovenden.'

David raised his eyebrows and wrote it down. 'What was his address?'

'The same as mine, in Southgrove,' she said faintly, then gathering her forces as indigation smote her for the position she had been somehow got into, she said in a stronger voice, 'It's a boarding-house. We, Noel and I, and five other people, lived there. Mrs. Venny was a good landlady. If you want her address, I suppose I'll have to give it to you, but she won't like it. She used to say that a boarding-house had to keep itself to itself, never have sick people in it or the need to call the police. She'd hate to have her address given even indirectly to the police.'

'Well, we'll leave it at 'Noel Ovenden, staying at the house of a Mrs. Venny in Southgrove'.' The police could easily check up on that information. 'And why couldn't this Mr. Ovenden take the package himself, or better still, send it through the post? My dear, it is possible to insure, register or otherwise cover the value of a thing going through the post nowadays.'

'I don't know why. He telephoned me when I was on the station. I don't know where he was. He said the London train was in and I must hurry or I'd miss it, and I had to pick up the ticket and packet at the ticket office. They were holding them out to me. And someone held open a door of the train and I fell in practically. It was as rushed as that. That's why I haven't any luggage. I didn't intend to stay in London.' Not then, but it had been in her mind, hadn't it? And the thought was so clearly mirrored on her face that David watching her, saw it, and wondered.

'Where was he telephoning from? How did you know he was on the telephone?'

'A porter gave me a written message, to say go into a callbox and phone a number.'

'The telephone number of Mrs. Venny's house, or perhaps his office? Where did he work, by the way?'

'Oh, does it matter? No, neither of those. Actually it was a number a bit like the one in the callbox where I was,' she said, thinking, and she sounded surprised. So, David thought, her brain is working well enough, if at a slower pace than usual, perhaps.

'And didn't you ask him where he was calling from?' David asked, thinking. 'Or how he should know you'd be in the station?'

She leaned forward holding her head

in her hands. 'I can't tell you any more, otherwise I shall have to tell you everything, and you won't believe it.'

'Well, I find it hard to believe on the facts I have, so perhaps you'd better tell me everything.'

'You think I'm out of my mind!' she accused him.

'Indeed I don't. If . . . ' and he paused to choose his words with care. 'If I were a policeman asking you these questions and getting these answers, I might be tempted to think you were either not telling the truth or keeping a whole lot of the truth back. But I would never think there was anything wrong with your brain,' and he smiled. 'The thing is, you don't trust me, do you?'

'I'm glad you don't think I'm going crazy, because I was beginning to wonder if I was, because of the way everyone looked at me, on the train, after the train had gone, here in your house. And no, I don't think I do trust . . . not just you, but anyone. I don't know. It's because of the things that have been happening to me, since . . . two days ago.'

'Two days ago. Now you are intriguing me. Well, before my telephone rings and calls me out,' he smiled, 'put my mind at rest. Put me out of my misery. Take your back hair down and tell me everything. Go on, you'll feel better.'

It was very tempting. She actually nodded and drew a deep breath, when a heavy tread sounded up the path, and just before the front door bell rang they both caught a glimpse of what could only be a policeman's uniform.

Her heart beat fit to suffocate her, as David got up and went to the door. The policeman knew him. 'I got your information quicker than I thought, and I was going off duty and thought I'd pop it in in case it was urgent.'

'You've checked the names?' David sounded as excited as if it had been him.

'Well, that's just it. In the first place, there's no record of this Miss or Mrs. Quorn — not even on the Voting Lists. And in the second place, which I can personally vouch for, since Pillerwick is my home town, there is no such place as Challeybourn Street. Not even a little new street pushed in between a gap in the houses — I checked that too, just to make sure.'

'And this Nurse Lemira Jeacock?'

'That will take a little longer, but so far, no joy.'

'They could be assumed names, I suppose,' David said hopefully.

'The first might,' the policeman said doubtfully. 'But a nurse's name? No, no way.'

4

Judy collapsed. The local hospital was full. The few beds they reserved for casualty couldn't be used for such a thing. The nearest hospital that could take her was so far away that the doctor's mother urged him to let her stay in their house. 'I'll look after her, and you can treat her, David. Besides, I get the odd feeling that this girl won't be safe if she goes out of our hands. I don't know why, but she tells such an odd story yet I believe her.'

'You believe a story about people who don't even exist, mother?'

'I want to know what happened to her this morning. She started to tell you, you said, and never got any further. David, do let's keep her here.' And when her son looked as if he were going to demur on principle, she said, 'David, I keep thinking . . . it might be

104

your sister. Oh, I know she's married and got a husband to look after her, but before she married, and worked in London, I used to worry about her. Every time I read about some young girl getting involved in something queer that we never heard the last of in the newspapers, I used to think of the most awful things. It might be my daughter, I used to think, and there were times when I couldn't bear it. Has this girl got a mother who is worrying about her?'

'Okay, okay Mother, I know when I'm beaten,' he said with a smile. Do as you like! I'll telephone Sergeant Neville and tell him what's developed. There's another one who'd like to see her kept here under his nose.'

'I read a story the other day about a young girl who was the tail end of something big and frightful and nobody listened to her and . . . '

'Mother! Now that's going too far! No stories you've been reading, please! The thing is, with private nursing and care, we'll get her back on even keel again where she won't be frightened and anxious, and you may find its a case of an importuning boy-friend or losing a job and being alone in the world. Something that seems simple and straightforward to us, but can be purely terrifying to someone young and unhappy.' And he frowned as he said it. She was so young and curiously untouched. Vulnerable, he thought. And why was he getting worked up about her? He had young and pretty and untouched girls on his list of patients but they didn't really cause him to lose any sleep over them although he did his best for them. But Judy Henderson was different, and it bothered him. He was a sensible chap; he prided himself on being just that. Medium good at his work, medium good at almost everything. Nothing outstanding, except perhaps in being comfortable in his own quiet corner. He had been very good at that, until Judy Henderson had burst into his life. Now, in the space of a few hours, everything was looking oddly different.

Impatiently he left everything to his mother, picked up his bag and went out on his rounds. In his ears his mother's last words: 'I'm glad you didn't send her to that big hospital near Birmingham. It's too big; too impersonal. I would worry about her there, although I know it was the only one with free beds at this moment.' A fine thing when his own mother started worrying about a complete stranger!

★ ★ ★

He had a full surgery the next day, and his round was bloated. Yet he couldn't get Judy out of his mind. She lay very white and still in his sister's bedroom. Like the late Miss Remington, he found that still face fascinating because it was so hard to describe. Even without the myriad emotions flitting across it, it was a 'taking' face. His mother at the end of the bed murmured, 'Funny, I feel as if she'd been under our roof for some time. She doesn't feel like a stranger.'

But she was a stranger, a stranger with a great question mark over her. While she lay like that, in the narrow bed in his sister's pretty little room, several things happened. The police finished checking for the nurse's name and confirmed that there was no such nurse as Lemira Jeacock. They also confirmed that there was no sign of a person having been thrown from that train.

They had also checked Judy's story (received from the doctor) that a ticket to London had been bought for her, and a packet left with it. The clerk hadn't been inquisitive enough (and probably much too busy) to notice what the address was on the packet, though he did remember seeing it was written in thick black block capital letters on a white label. The clerk described the man who had brought the ticket and left the packet with it. Neither young nor middle-aged, very ordinary in fact.

No distinguishing things such as spectacles, moustache or anything like that. So ordinary he wouldn't recognise him if he was to see him again.

But a ticket to London had been bought for her and the packet had been left for her. And now she had been robbed of it.

Or had she? The police were wondering if she had delivered it to someone on the train and was just saying she had been robbed.

He took the tray of hot milk up to Judy when his mother said she was awake. He took her pulse and temperature and said she could sit up. She seemed glad of the hot milk, but very much put out at the trouble she said they had gone to.

'You mean, staying here? Don't you like it? We did try to get you into a hospital. Well, better nursing and treatment. But they were all full up.' And having deliberately said that, he waited for and noticed the sharp alarm in her eyes at the thought of being in a hospital.

'As soon as I can,' she said carefully,

'I must find a job. I haven't got one now. I must find a job.'

'If you'll only disclose this Mrs. Venny's address, I could send for your luggage. You'll want your things.'

'Oh, no, please don't — she'd want a month's rent in lieu of notice and I — well, I have got it in the Post Office, but until I can get out — '

'That's all right. I'll see to that for you, and fetch your luggage, and you can repay me later,' he said easily, but this brought on such panic.

'No, please no!' She even held on to his hand so tightly that her nails dug into his flesh. 'I don't want anyone to know where I am — not while I'm in bed, not able to move away. Please!'

'Well, I don't know, don't you think it would be courteous to let the young man know his package hadn't been delivered? He must have rated it highly to go to the expense of buying a ticket for someone to deliver it. And why couldn't he have taken it himself, come to that?'

She shrugged. 'He had a job. I hadn't.'

'And he was friendly enough to be able to call on you at a moment's notice to do this for him?'

'Dr. Marland — ' she began.

'Oh, goodness, if we're going to be so formal, how can I ask you all the searching questions I intend to?' he smiled. 'Besides, you're a guest in my mother's house. She calls you Judy, I know, so I will too, and that means you must call me David.'

'I can't do that!' she protested. 'Well, because — well, I was going to tell you everything when that policeman came, and you'll hate me when you hear.'

'Well, you'll have to progress along that exciting road now. You can't just not continue, can you? I'll die of suspense.'

'Now you're laughing at me. And it's no laughing matter.'

'Prove it to me.'

She put the milk down. Her hands were shaking too badly to hold it any longer. 'My sort of job is being a secretary companion. Or going out from typing pools to do any odd secretarial job,' she said, very slowly. 'Sometimes for old ladies. Well, they keep dying.'

His smile vanished, but he merely said quietly, 'Go on.'

'What I mean is, the first one fell out of her window, trying to get her cat in off a ledge. But nobody but me saw it happen. It was only my word. Noel said he'd tell people, if I didn't do what he wanted about the documents.'

'Tell people *what*?'

'Tell them that it was only my word that I saw it from down below because I hadn't really arrived for work. I suppose he found out (he does seem to be able to find out) that her relatives expected to find more valuables in the house — nobody was accused, of course, but they might have thought that I . . . '

'Take it easy. Now let's get back to the documents. What documents?'

'Noel had some documents he wanted Miss Remington, the last old lady, my last job, in Southgrove, you understand — he wanted her to sign them. I kept telling him she wouldn't sign anything she didn't understand. He said I was to slip them in between her letters when she was signing them. But it wouldn't have worked. Anyway, the morning I took them to the house, I wasn't really meaning to do anything about them, but I couldn't, anyway, because she was lying dead, near the front door.'

He frowned. 'When was this?' So she told him. The fateful morning of the train incident. 'Yesterday . . . it seems years ago.'

'And what happened then?' so she strove to tell him. Little short breathless sentences.

About the Peke, lying dead. About the birds, silent, still covered. About the necklace in the Buddha and how she had come to know it was there. Everything, right up to the finding of the new key in her bag.

Of course he pounced on that. 'Now just a minute! How could a new key get into a girl's handbag without her knowing? I may be a bachelor, but I have a sister who has taught me that no matter how much a woman bungs out her handbag she usually knows what's in it at all times, because she's always scrabbling in the darned thing!'

'I had put it on the table in the hall while I went upstairs to see . . . who was up there. Well, I thought at first it looked a bit like Noel. Someone could have been in the house and popped it in my bag.'

He wouldn't accept that. So she had to tell him everything else. About the second visit, and the way she found the drawer forced in the Buddha. 'When I went to the solicitors with the cat basket, I did try to tell him about it but he didn't want to stop. He told me to leave everything to them. All was in order. I couldn't force him to listen.'

'Why didn't you tell his secretary? She evidently wanted to listen?'

'For the same reason,' Judy said firmly, 'that I am now wishing with all my heart that I didn't start telling you. Because she wouldn't have believed me. Any more than you do.'

How he wished he could have had his mother there listening, but they had both decided that he must talk to Judy alone; she wouldn't talk before a second party, they had both been sure.

'It's not that I don't believe you, my dear. It's just that coupled with the story of the body falling out of the train, it is all such a fantastic saga, the sort of thing that is highly improbable to have happened all to one young woman in one day of her life.'

'And I haven't told you about the man in the zip jacket who was following me, nor the way I think the intruder got into the house, nor . . . '

There was a movement at the door and his mother came in. 'I don't think it's a fantastic story,' she said warmly, to Judy. 'I've been unashamedly listening, my dear, and I want to hear all the other things. Everything you can think of. Don't take any notice of my son.

Men tend to prefer to believe themselves too practical to believe anything that is at all extraordinary. But I'm not like that. I think life is not ordinary at all! Do tell me how the intruder got into the house. I've been racking my brains, because I'm sure you're like me, about locking everything up when you leave a place.'

So Judy told her. 'But you see, it looks as if all the attics in that terrace are interconnecting, so how could one find out which house he used.'

David, of course, couldn't believe such a thing. 'Judy, nobody would leave a hole in the attic like that! No house would be burglar-proof!'

'Well, we could find out why they were like that, or if someone enterprising had knocked out a few bricks,' his mother said soothingly, and elicited more information from Judy. 'I expect you don't remember where you were to have delivered the packet, do you? With all this happening.'

'Yes, I do. It was to a Mr. Rosenberg

in Hatton Garden.'

That stunned them both. They stared at Judy in such a way that her hand flew to her mouth. 'The diamond necklace? Oh, no, Noel couldn't — ' but hadn't that thought flashed into her own mind at the start of that train journey.

'You liked this Noel person rather a lot, didn't you?' Mrs. Marland said gently. 'Were you engaged to marry him?'

Judy nodded miserably. 'At least, I never had a ring but he was always too broke to buy one, and I said why did we bother. It was a needless expense.'

'So you were just going to be married quietly, and both go on working? I thought you might. I always feel so sorry for the young these days. Money never seems to come in enough quantities. I suppose he was a clerk in the office of the solicitors?' she probed with gentleness.

Judy said, 'Oh, no, of course he wasn't. He was in an office, sort of importers. Jason and Wildman of River Lane. You can check that too!' she said fiercely to David, who said calmly, writing it down,

'I will. At least, I'll give it to the police. I'll have to, won't I?' he said, as he met her indignant look.

'He was a smart mick, I'll own, but he wouldn't do anything bad!'

'I can't wait to meet this Noel Ovenden,' the doctor said with relish.

Judy slept for many hours, without knowing that she had been given something to make her sleep. She only knew that when she awoke, for a moment everything seemed fine, until the memory of past events came rushing back to her.

'What day is it?' she asked the doctor's mother.

She gave the date collectedly, and waited for the explosion. 'You mean I've been out for the count for three days?'

'On and off, my dear. It's done you a lot of good. My son has a lot of faith in inducing sleep for certain things, particularly for people who have been through what you have!'

'Then you did believe all I told you?'

'Well, some of it,' she said slowly.

'But not about the diamond necklace

worth thousands which was stolen from the Buddha?' Judy thrust.

'Oh, as to that, I never gave it another thought,' Mrs. Marland said, with a frown. 'No, it was this young man you told us about. This Noel Ovenden.'

'What about him?'

'My son has friends in the local police force, as you know,' Mrs. Marland began.

'Don't I know it? He feeds them information like into a computer and back comes the answer, it doesn't exist!'

'Yes, well, the police have access to practically if not every detail one would want to know,' David's mother said. 'They can't trace your nurse nor the person who is reputed to have written to her a letter (which only you have seen) and the street you told us about just isn't in Pillerwick.'

'But what's this got to do with Noel?'

'Well, they found Mrs. Venny's boarding house but I'm afraid they say your Noel doesn't exist, either.'

5

There was a long silence. David's mother squeezed Judy's hand anxiously.

Judy dragged her eyes back from the middle distance. Her face felt stiff. She said, 'What do you do, when you've been going around with a man, been made love to by him, been promised marriage to him, lent him money, betrayed your employer's business to him, done things at an instant's notice for him because you were afraid of his temper, and then been soothed back to comfortable relations with him again, by his charm and his clever tongue. He was a real person, Mrs. Marland. And now you tell me the police say he doesn't exist! What do you expect me to do — or say?'

'Oh, my dear,' David's mother said faintly.

David came in at that moment. The

door to Judy's room had been open and he had heard her outburst as he came up the stairs.

Looking back afterwards, he was inclined to think that this was the moment when he began to feel differently towards Judy. If one can ever pinpoint the exact moment in one's feelings, man for woman, when the turning point arrives, then this was it. He had arranged with his mother to do something that had tipped the scale and here was a possible danger point. He felt he had been not only clumsy, a bad doctor, but needlessly cruel. As he watched Judy's face, he was afraid. He wanted to take her in his arms, cuddle her and tell her to forget it. There must be some mistake. He had not asked the right questions of Judy. Or perhaps it was Mrs. Venny, lying to the police for some reason. Judy had said the woman was almost pathologically against dealings with the police. But now he was afraid to do anything in case at this delicate stage it would be the wrong thing to do.

A frozen look crept over that delicate face of Judy's, and she wasn't even listening to the soothing things his mother was saying. She stared out of the window, and for a moment he felt a fear that she wouldn't bring her mind back to them.

His mother terminated the awful moment by being her own sensible self. She said briskly, 'Well, that's the news! I must say, my dear, I'm glad you're out of that boarding house and under my roof. I cannot feel it was a good place for you to be in, for quite clearly that woman is not telling the truth. There is something very odd going on, although it may not necessarily concern you! Meantime, what am I thinking of? The first thing one does for the patient is — a wash, and then light food. A fine nurse I am!'

Perhaps the word 'nurse' was the one in all that, which reached Judy. It was an effort to bring herself back, to this room and the two people in it, but she did. 'Nurse?' she repeated, and briefly horror filled her eyes again.

David said, 'Yes, nurse.' He sat down by the bed, where his mother had been sitting, and took Judy's hands. 'You know, I can't help having the odd sort of feeling that they were a lot of young people having a joke on that train. They will do it, you know, without thought of who they will hurt.'

'What young people?' she asked dully.

'The young men you said were jostling in the place near the train door and you were held from behind while they closed in on that girl in the nurse's coat.'

'She *was* a nurse,' Judy said flatly.

'How do you know? Did she tell you about her training, anything that would make her different from just anyone announcing that she was a nurse?'

Judy thought. 'The thing is, I couldn't understand a lot of what she was saying because of the odd way she talked, and the way she kept dropping her voice and looking nervously over her shoulder when people went by. But I got the impression — '

'That's what I mean!' David said, in a pleased way. 'Now supposing she was saying she was a nurse — '

'Why would she do that?'

'I don't know. But to be honest, there doesn't seem to be much reason why she did any of the things she did. Why would she tell a lot of her private business to a complete stranger or show a complete stranger a letter she said was threatening?' he reasoned.

'Because she was worried sick. About something. I may have got the reason wrong in her garbled account, but she was worried sick. No doubt about that. And scared too. Scared of making the trip to the loo.'

'Is that reasonable? If you'd been scared of your life, would you have — ' he began, but she said, in that queer flat voice, 'I was scared of my life. I told you. Well, if I didn't, I meant to. I don't know! I was being followed. Before I got on the train. When Noel asked me to go to London with that packet, I let myself be rushed because I was glad to go. Glad to get away from that man.'

'What man, my dear?' David asked, with a glance at his mother.

'Doesn't matter. He didn't follow me on to the train. So why do we have to talk about it? Nobody will believe me. Well, if you don't believe Noel existed, what's the use of anything?' And there she had him. It really was no use pursuing the matter further.

Not to her. But he would talk to his friend the sergeant. If only he could persuade the sergeant to question her. But as the police now told him, why would they question her? They had searched for a young man named Noel Ovendcn, and he simply wasn't anywhere. David hadn't told Judy, but the police had not found him on the voting list, either, nor in any of the import offices. They had combed them all, because David, who was also a doctor, had been so insistent. The girl was his patient, he said. And she had claimed seeing a murder (and they could find no body, no witnesses, no suitcase belonging to a nurse that no one had seen, a nurse whose name was not anywhere, either, and who had shown Judy a letter from a non-existent person in a non-existent street) and Judy had claimed to be robbed of a packet, the contents of which were unknown to her and which she had insisted had been given to her to deliver by this young man who didn't exist. Moreover, he hadn't given it to her personally but had left it with the booking clerk at the station, who didn't know the man who had left it and whose description was worse than useless.

David's friend the sergeant suggested gently that this young woman might have been involved in an accident, and was a little befuddled. It was a kind way of putting it, David thought. He might be suggesting Judy was suffering from hallucinations, or was perhaps just another of those people who go into the police station and make a wild assertion which the police must follow up but which comes to nothing. Sensation mongers, or perhaps just people who are lonely and want to be given some attention.

He left things to his mother. She took Judy out shopping with her, as soon as she was fit to get up, and she introduced Judy to her friends. But she was distressed to find that Judy was always looking behind her, as if she still expected to be followed.

The next day she lost Judy, and found her coming out of a telephone booth. 'I wish you'd tell me, dear, if you want to go off and do something different. I was worried about you,' Mrs. Marland said.

Judy apologised gracefully. 'It just came over me. I just had to telephone to . . . Noel.' She swallowed. 'At his office.'

Mrs. Marland's smile wouldn't stay pinned to her face. She did force herself to sound fairly normal as she asked, 'What happened? Did you manage to speak to him?'

'You didn't really expect a 'yes' in

answer to that, did you, Mrs. Marland?'
Judy asked savagely. 'I made two
telephone calls. One to Mrs. Venny and
one to his office. Jason and Wildman's,
where he always said he worked.'

'But I thought it was now established
that nobody knows where he worked,
dear!'

'I agree — I've even tried their
number; but he once gave me another
telephone number where I could get
him.'

'And did you . . . get any satisfaction
from either call, dear?' David's mother
asked gently.

'It depends on what you mean by
satisfaction, doesn't it?' Judy asked, still
in that angry tone. 'Mrs. Venny
screamed at me. I have never heard her
behave like that before. She said, 'Oh,
it's you! I might have known you'd be
at the bottom of this! I don't know what
you're playing at, miss, bringing the
police to my house to find a man I've
never heard of, but I won't forget it.
And don't you forget there's rent owing

in lieu of notice and I've got your things and you won't get them back until you come here and settle with me'.'

'Oh, dear. You must let David go back and tidy that end for you, dear. What about the other telephone call?'

At first, she thought Judy wasn't going to answer. When she did, Judy said, 'I don't understand it. I suppose I thought it would be a friend's house. A horrible man answered. He sounded drunk. There was a lot of noise in the background. Things falling, harsh voices. He said he didn't know what I was talking about, and he swore at me and hung up.' She stared down the end of the long street. 'I won't believe it. I'm not losing my mind. I'm not! But why are perfectly normal people behaving like this to me?'

David's mother hastily gave her something to do which required some concentration, certainly in crossing that busy road. And she concentrated herself on talking fast about everything under the sun except Judy's telephone calls.

But David, when he heard about it, was rather glum.

That evening was David's mother's night for going to a neighbour's house for their weekly gathering to knit blanket patches. Why she couldn't do it at home, David didn't know. But his mother was a widow and he never stopped her going out to meet friends, because of the surgery. But that night he really needed help, with a boy whose mother was inept at holding him for an injection. Previously David's mother had helped, but the woman hadn't said she was coming tonight. An evening surgery was rather late for a child of his age, and David thought despairingly of the struggle ahead, and of the possible damage the boy might do. He could have blessed Judy when she opened the surgery door a few inches from the house side and looked in enquiringly. 'I heard shrieks. Can I help?' she said in her clear little voice.

David was pithy. 'Yes, *please!*' he said, and nodded to a white overall hanging behind the door. 'Put that on, would you?'

She was quick and precise. 'Tell me what to do,' she said, so he did, and much to his surprise she was more than adequate, holding the boy firmly and without fuss. She stayed and helped with getting cards out of the filing index. He had forgotten she had done secretarial work.

After surgery, he stood up and stretched. Then he put his hands on his hips, surveyed her with a smile, and said, 'Well! You're better than my mother at quelling a rough house! How about taking on the job?'

'If you think I can, I'd like to,' she said, without particular emotion.

He nodded. He would feel better if he knew she was beside him. He, too, had noticed the way she looked round continually when she was in the street. Had someone really been following her, he wondered uneasily?

So it fell into a pattern, Judy helping him in surgery, and going out with him on his rounds, sitting in the car while he went into the house unless he needed help in dealing with a patient. He was glad to know someone was sitting in his car. Some of the streets were in the poor part, where boys would quite casually run a coin along the side of the car, scraping the paintwork. Already he had run up two sizeable bills having the panels re-sprayed They would have been even bigger if the man who had done the job for him hadn't been a one-time patient and reduced the size of the bill by way of gratitude. In a place like Axwood, that sort of thing wasn't unknown. In one short week she had slid neatly into his life.

It was one day on such a trip that he had come out to the car and found her sitting with sun glasses on, though the day was dull, and her bright hair completely hidden under something which the startled David could only think was remarkably like the piece of rag he kept for cleaning the condensation off the inside of the windscreen. As it was missing from the glove compartment, it strengthened his conviction that that was its identity.

Judy glanced at him and saw what he was looking at. 'It was all I could find to cover my hair,' she said. 'I'll never come out without a scarf or something, again. Never!'

'But why do you want to hide that beautiful hair?' he asked, trying to keep his voice light, but suddenly feeling abject dismay.

'*He* was coming along! The man I told you about, the one in the zippered jacket. I saw him, a long way back, in the mirror. It was that, or hiding under the blanket, and — well, this seemed easier and better.'

And she was shaking again.

David said, 'Well, we've finished the rounds. Let's go home and have something to eat. That's your trouble. Empty! The old tummy plays up like the devil with some people. I know — it does with me!'

'You mean it makes you think

someone is following you?' she asked quietly.

'No, it just makes me feel like being violent with anyone in my way — I just make a bee-line for food. Come on, let's go,' and he started up the car and drove home more quickly than she had ever seen him do before.

When he told his mother, she said thoughtfully, 'It can't be hallucinations, David. She's so normal otherwise.'

He thoughtfully regarded his mother, who hastened to explain further. 'Well, what I mean is, we find her stories improbable and think she's making them up. Now let's look at the other side of it; suppose she's telling the truth and these things do happen to her. How does that strike you? It would mean that a perfectly normal girl is having odd things happen to her . . . '

'But why? Why should such things happen to her? It won't wash, Mother.'

They stared helplessly at each other. They were both extremely practical people. Nothing fanciful ever occurred to either of them. To be faced by the thought that such things were really happening to someone, was unacceptable. Even David's mother, who had made the suggestion, didn't really believe it.

Judy came in at that moment, and looked extremely upset. She was carrying a newspaper. 'I found it in the waiting-room. I was tidying up. They leave all sorts of things. There's a pair of spectacles in a case,' she said, holding it out. 'No name inside. There was, but it's got rubbed off.'

'Well, don't worry, my dear. I think I recognise them as old Mrs. Jones's. She'll send someone round for them when she remembers where she left them,' David said, and his mother added, 'I'll pop round with them. She might need them for some sewing.'

'I'm not worried about them. It's this,' and she held out the paper, which carried the banner: *Southgrove Daily Chronicle*. She indicated the Obituary Coloumn. 'It wasn't like that! They've made it sound as if she collapsed by her chair in her parlour, not the way I found her, lying at the bottom of the stairs.'

David took it and read it, his mother reading over his shoulder. 'Well, it doesn't actually say that,' David pointed out. 'It doesn't say where she was found, either. But it sounds a perfectly normal thing, and it doesn't sound as if the old lady had very much in the way of valuables.'

'It's a conspiracy!' Judy burst out. 'I've a good mind to telephone that paper and tell them just what did happen!'

David said, after a silence, 'You know, we've only heard a very patchy account from you, my dear. I've got a little while. Why don't we sit down and you answer some questions, as it gives me a better idea of it all?'

'You want to hush me up, like everyone else,' Judy said.

'Indeed I don't. If the old lady really met with foul play, then I shall be the first to — '

' — contact your friend, the police sergeant?' Judy retorted. 'Don't bother

— don't bother! He'll just say it's out of his district, and he'll contact the South-grove police and they'll say, oh, dear, that daft girl who's searching for some-one called Noel Ovenden who doesn't exist! Oh, don't bother, Dr. Marland!'

'I thought we'd got to Christian name terms,' David said mildly.

'And so we had,' Judy said passion-ately. 'All right, I'm being rude to two kind people who are giving me shelter and not taking a penny from me, so I'll do what you want me to do. But I can assure you, from my experience since three days before Miss Remington died, that I know perfectly well what will happen. I shall see your two faces set in that same look that I've seen on the faces of other people. And I . . . I don't think I could bear it.'

David took her hand, and was surprised at the emotion that touch aroused in him. He took it that he seriously thought she was deranged and the future frightened him. He held her hand more firmly. He was a doctor, wasn't he? No one else had affected him like this? Why couldn't he treat her as just another patient? But he couldn't. He let her hand go, and stood up, and put his hands in his pockets, and he missed the quick look of comprehension on his mother's face.

They questioned Judy, and she answered them, patiently, even putting in some things she thought of herself.

At the end, David asked her, 'Why didn't you insist on that old fogey of a solicitor listening to you? Weren't you really sure that it had been a necklace worth a fortune? Could you tell a good piece if you saw it?'

'I think so. The setting was . . . rather special. Not like in a cheap necklace. You know what I mean. It had been neglected, of course. But it caught the light in the stones, even in that dingy room.'

'And the other necklace you saw there later — that didn't?'

She shook her head. 'No, it didn't look, didn't even feel, the same. I'm not specific enough, am I? I know I'm vague. It's just — well, I feel things are the way they are. I have impressions, and I don't believe they are necessarily wrong. It's all a bit peculiar . . . as if what's happening is just a bit above my head. Those documents Noel wanted signed. I don't know what they are. I did read some of them, though I was a bit rushed and I don't understand legal documents. They sounded sort of legal language and they sounded a bit well, threatening, but they went on and on and I couldn't get at what they were.'

'But the only thing he'd want her to sign, to be of use to him, surely, would be a Power of Attorney, and that would announce itself, clearly, at the top.'

'Yes, I thought of that. But you see, it didn't make sense. The thing is, he said persuade her to sign them, but I couldn't have. Nobody could have. She wasn't the sort to be intimidated.'

David and his mother exchanged glances. 'How do you know that, Judy?'

'Well, she was . . . belligerent. People

didn't like her so her attitude was, well, tell them to go to the devil, she didn't care. She didn't let anyone bully her. But . . . she did admit to being afraid, that last day. She said someone was getting in the house, moving her things, taking some things. But she wouldn't tell me what she'd lost. That was when she showed me the necklace. But she made me turn away so I couldn't see how she opened or closed the drawer. But she was right — someone got in and removed the real thing and put rubbish in its place, and the drawer had been forced.'

David made up his mind. 'Let me ask my friend the sergeant to question you and tell him all this, will you, Judy?' But she wouldn't. She was tired, and she shrank from having anyone else look at her as if she were making it all up.

'You don't really believe me about the necklace, do you?' she asked David.

Before he could answer, his mother said, 'Look, I've got a better idea. David, we really haven't thought enough about

Judy's two telephone calls that day when we were out,' and she went over them again, though he couldn't see anything of special significance in them. 'I know, I agree,' his mother said. 'But what I thought was, if you were to go over to that Mrs. Venny's place and settle for Judy's things and bring them away, and ask the woman if Judy ever had a man friend. You might catch her on the wrong foot and make her decide to tell the truth.'

David said, 'Yes, I've been thinking I'd like to visit Southgrove. I want to see the solicitors, too. They might listen to a man saying there was (or had been) something of value there in that little idol. But we are rather stuck, you know. If, as Judy seems to think, the real necklace was in that packet she was supposed to take to Hatton Garden, then she was in possession of stolen property — '

'But she wasn't to know that!' his mother put in swiftly.

'Well, no, I suppose one might say

that. But anyway, it got stolen in the melee . . . hey, that's an idea. If those young thugs knew about the necklace all that business of the nurse being thrown out of the window could have been laid on. How does that strike anyone?'

They thought about it, then David's mother said, 'There would seem to have been a fair number of them in it including the one who took it. Would the proceeds be worth it? And again, if they did throw the nurse out of the window — '

'Could they have thrown a dummy out of the window, dressed as a nurse, and meantime that girl could have slipped into the next compartment, while Judy was struggling with those chaps?' David asked, looking enthusiastic.

His mother was dubious. 'That would mean more people further down the line to pick up the dummy before the train was stopped and anyone saw it. Besides a dummy wouldn't be as heavy as a human body, if one is thinking in terms of one of those dummies in shop windows with clothes on, surely?'

Judy covered her ears. 'Oh, don't! Besides, it couldn't be. I saw her go out of the window. I did, I did!' She looked piteous. 'And she screamed. Oh, how she screamed. I'll never forget it as long as I live.'

'But what happened to her then?' David couldn't help voice his thoughts.

His mother said, 'I'm thinking. David, isn't there a drug, given orally, that makes a person vulnerable to suggestion — you know, they believe what is set up to be happening, even though it might not be?'

He looked keenly at her. Judy said, 'What's that supposed to mean? If you mean have I had any injections lately, no, I haven't.'

'It's given orally, on sugar. Some people have them that way if they can't take injections,' his mother said, but Judy shook her head. 'No, I saw it, I saw it, and if you make me believe otherwise, I don't know what I'll do.'

They left her alone then, and she seemed calm enough after tea, when she insisted on helping David in surgery.

The next evening David's mother said she was going to the church to help lay out the stalls for the Sale of Work. 'David, could you manage without Judy? She tells me she's never seen this sort of thing got ready before.'

'Okay,' he grinned. 'The boy is not coming tonight, and so far as I know, it will be a fairly light surgery.'

'Oh, good, because I really would like to go,' she said, with more enthusiasm than they had yet seen from her. Her smile made his heart stand still. His mother caught sight of the great tenderness in his eyes as he stared back at Judy, and she caught her breath in alarm. She had persuaded herself on that other occasion that David was not really wanting to be interested in Judy. Now she saw that he was unable to help himself. It was a thing she didn't want. Judy was a dear child and she wanted to be responsible for her but she really didn't want her son to be thinking of this girl with the unknown background to be his wife. Was she hurt in her mind or was she making an elaborate pretence, or had she suffered some dreadful experience which was making her, in spite of herself, believe strange things happened all the time?

'Isn't David nice?' Judy said, almost dancing along beside her. 'You must be very happy to have such a nice kind man for your son, Mrs. Marland!'

David's mother lost her breath with surprise. This was a new slant on Judy. She said faintly, 'Indeed I am most happy, my dear!'

'Has he never thought of being married?' Judy asked absently, looking up at the church as they neared it. She liked what she saw. It had a creeper all over its porch and tower, and was what she thought of as a cosy looking church. There were nicely kept lawns and weed-free paths around it, and the people going in to prepare for the Sale of Work looked friendly people, like

David's mother.

'Why do you ask, Judy?' Mrs. Marland said, but Judy merely looked astonished at her, as if she had already lost the thread of the conversation.

Someone came up and Mrs. Marland needed to introduce Judy, and the moment was lost. Whether Judy was getting interested in David or whether it was merely a random question, she had no means of telling.

Yet the girl proved an asset that evening. She had plenty of good ideas though she didn't thrust herself forward, and she was more than willing to do anything to help other people. She confessed she had enjoyed herself very much as they left the church with a group of Mrs. Marland's friends.

One by one the other women left them with a cheerful goodnight, and in the end there were just David's mother and Judy, walking along the tree-lined avenue off the main road of shops. Judy said, 'Still early yet. Will David have finished surgery? I had thought of

146

asking him if he'd like me to tidy his files for him. It is, after all, my special thing,' she smiled.

David's mother didn't have a chance to answer that happy reflection for Judy's smile froze on her face and her eyes widened in horror. David's mother followed her glance and saw she was staring at a man coming down the path from the surgery; a man with dark hair, and wearing a zippered jacket. His hand was heavily bandaged. Mrs. Marland was about to say it was just one of the patients, although she hadn't seen him before, when she felt Judy break away from her and turned to see her running madly back the way they had come.

'Judy!' she called, and turned to run after her, but thought to look round at the man who had caused all this consternation. He must have heard Judy's running footsteps and heard Mrs. Marland call out to her, and it would, she thought, have been natural for him to turn round in surprise to see what was happening. But he didn't. He kept steadily on until he reached a small van parked at the kerb on the other side of the street. He didn't look at the man at the wheel. He just got in, and the small van drove away.

It was with the greatest difficulty that Mrs. Marland persuaded Judy to come out from round the corner where she found her hiding, shivering, her hands pressed to her mouth.

David, who was closing the door on the last patient, saw what was happening and strolled down the road until he came to them. 'What's the matter?' he asked tautly, looking from Judy to his very bothered mother.

'It was that man who came out with the bandaged hand,' she explained. 'Judy thought he was following her.'

'Oh, don't be silly, Judy,' David said, trying to make light of it. 'He was not a regular patient but a bona fide one, I assure you. He had a badly cut hand. I had to stitch it, as a matter of fact.'

She shook her head and kept on shaking it. 'You don't understand. I don't care what he did to his hand, he is the man who was following me in Southgrove. I thought I'd escaped him on the train but I haven't. He's here, here in Axwood, and now he knows where I can be found. I thought I'd escaped him, but I haven't — I haven't!' she said, her voice rising sharply and her eyes registering terror. And nothing David or his mother could say would shake her on that point.

6

They went all over the story again and in the end David sedated Judy and insisted that his mother had a bed made up in Judy's room. His last words to Judy before her eye-lids closed wearily, were, '*If* that man were following you, I believe he'd take to wearing something less easy for you to remember. If a chap follows a person, he remains inconspicuous for obvious reasons. He wouldn't have come to *me* to stitch up his hand but found some other doctor in the town!'

It seemed an irrefutable argument, but now David's mother was uneasy. The girl had been so happy tonight. She began to glimpse something of Judy's nature before all this began happening.

The next day was David's half day and he said to his mother, 'What do you think of this for an idea? I want to go to Southgrove, to see some things for myself. How about my taking Judy with me?'

'If she'll go,' she said doubtfully.

Judy seemed to flinch openly when it was put to her. David said, 'It will be better if you come as well, to collect your things from Mrs. Venny's. She doesn't know me. She's hardly likely to part with them to me.' So Judy agreed.

As she stood there hesitating, David smiled and said, 'Now what are you thinking about?'

'Do you know exactly what happened when the police went there, or just that they asked about Noel and she said she didn't know such a person?' And as David frowned in perplexity, Judy said, 'Did they actually look at her book of lodgers — she has six men and myself.'

David stood up, looking keenly at her. 'I wonder what made you say that? As a matter of fact, they did, naturally, ask to see her book, and she showed it openly, I gather. And yes, there were six names of men, and one Miss Judy

Henderson. Why, Judy?'

'So there you are! One of them must have been Noel — well, even if he's not there now, and a new name in his place, his name would have been there at one time! Did they look?'

'Yes, they looked. Nobody had moved. The same names had been there since — oh, for a year or two at least,' David said slowly. They had had no nonsense about a man watching their house that day, which he had rather feared. Instead, Judy had thought up this mare's nest.

'I wonder,' she said, rather bitterly, 'why you told your mother yesterday that you didn't think those two telephone calls of mine were significant?'

He came over and took her arms, shaking her gently. 'You've gone all unfriendly. Why? And what does that remark of yours mean?'

'As if you didn't know,' she said, struggling to be free but without success. 'If you believed what was said, then Mrs. Venny remembered me but she didn't remember Noel, which is the most arrant nonsense.'

He didn't let her go. He pulled her to him and held her face against his chest and rubbed her hair. 'I wish you would let all this go,' he said softly. 'I don't know why you keep on about it. I'm hoping that when we can get your things here, and I've seen the solicitors and satisfied myself on one or two other points, we can shut the whole thing out of our minds, and you can stay on here and get back to — '

' — normal health?' she said, mockingly. 'You believe I'm going out of my mind, then, after all! Yes, you do — you must do! Or you wouldn't think we can shut off what's happened in Southgrove, forget it all and start afresh.'

But she did go with him, in spite of her animosity. She wanted her things and she wanted to see Mrs. Venney. And for the moment she seemed to have forgotten the experience of the man in the zippered jacket.

She directed him plainly and briefly to Mrs. Venny's road, too, once they had reached Southgrove, which was no mean feat, since the entrance to the town was almost a spaghetti junction. They passed the seedy wharves and buildings at the edge of its murky river, and he felt Judy's head turn that way as they passed. She was no doubt thinking of the man she knew as Noel Ovenden. He was so anxious to clear that business up that he didn't understand how it was that Judy couldn't see that his interest lay there and not with collecting her luggage. He was torn in two; he didn't want a Noel Ovenden to exist, because he would be the fiancé who would hold Judy to marriage. Yet he did want him to exist, because if he didn't, what state of mind did that indicate Judy was in?

He was surprised when she told him to stop. They were in a respectable road of tall Victorian houses, semi-detached and every bit of brass polished and every step either white or — if tiled

— then scrubbed clean. Its respectability forced him to accede to the picture she had drawn of Mrs. Venny, who was so proud of her boarding-house and didn't want police near. Judy squared her shoulders and marched up the steps beside him and when Mrs. Venny opened the door, Judy said smartly, before he could speak, 'I told you I'd attend to my luggage and rent as soon as I could, Mrs. Venny, and here I am to do that!'

He made a deprecating movement. He would have approached the matter more pacifically, but the neat little woman of uncertain though vigorous middle years, saw nothing strange in that outburst and merely sniffed and held the door wider for them to come in. 'This is Dr. Marland, at whose house I'm staying at the moment, with his mother!' Judy added firmly, which left nothing more to be said. Mrs. Venny said, 'Well, when I've seen your cash for the rent in lieu of notice — ' but Judy broke in, 'I am giving you the two weeks rent that I owe you and I would like my room kept here. There is no need for a month's rent in lieu of notice because I'm not certain whether I'll be leaving here or not.'

David looked at her in surprise but she didn't look his way. She didn't want to cut off this retreat, because she had no claim on David and his mother and she might want to leave if they didn't feel that the matter of her recent history had been cleared. Also she didn't want to draw everything out of her savings account, just to suit Mrs. Venny.

David, too, seemed comfortably off, and wouldn't understand what it felt like to have such a low level of savings in the Post Office and to want to keep it there. He thought he and his mother could stake her indefinitely.

Judy went upstairs with Mrs. Venny. It was a pity. He wanted to talk to Mrs. Venny alone. But Mrs. Venny didn't trust Judy to take everything from her room. She stayed to supervise the filling of one suitcase only, then they came downstairs together. David, meantime, had been shown into the front parlour and Judy went in to find him. Her glance, as always, went to the windows, and she cried out. 'Look! There he is! Look, Mrs. Venny — come here please! You've been asked about Noel Ovenden. Well, *there* he is!' and she pointed to a young man who was, David thought in fascination, about the most difficult person in the world to describe. Not good-looking yet not plain; not particularly dark or particularly fair. He supposed the young man might be acceptable in a young woman's eyes for he was dressed neatly, again in such formal fashion it would be difficult to say what he had on. No wonder Judy had been on the look-out for him, to point him out!

Mrs. Venny came to the window and looked, bridling as she thought of the visit of the police when that name had been bandied. And when she saw the young man who was crossing the road, she snorted angrily: 'What is this, miss, might I ask? I don't know what your game is but you know very well that

that's my Mr. Nolan!'

Judy swung round. 'I think you're mad too! That's my boy-friend! Do you deny that?' to which Mrs. Venny replied smartly, 'I do not, since I was never asked, nor wouldn't want to, since you were always hanging round him though what he saw in you I cannot think and I haven't noticed him crying his eyes out since you went away!'

Judy ignored all that. She turned to David. 'You see? I don't know what's going on but she does agree he's my boy-friend, the one I told you about!'

She didn't seem to notice how pained David was looking. This was the man in Judy's life, then. He did exist. This was the man he had heard Judy talking about to his mother; a man who had occupied her life so completely that he had left a hole, and almost sent her crazy when people wouldn't admit that he existed. David only prayed that Judy wouldn't ask outright if 'Nolan' was one of the names the police had found in the list in the guest book. He would have to tell her that it was, and there was still so much to be explained. He couldn't wait to hear how it was that his beloved Judy had thought of this man as Noel Ovenden when his landlady had entered him in her official list of lodgers under quite another name.

Judy hadn't even stayed with him. She had gone to the the street door and as the young man came up the path, she opened it to him. David was most anxious to see his expression when he saw Judy. But closely as he watched, from the bay window which gave an excellent view, that face of his barely flickered. If one could say it was a change of expression it was so minute as to defy description. Certainly one couldn't pin surprise, pleasure or dismay to it. And then Judy's voice: 'Noel! Do come in — There's so much I want to say but first, something must be cleared up!' and David went to the door of the room in time to see her take the young man's hand and almost drag him in.

He said, in an ordinarily pleasant

voice, 'Judy, whatever's the matter?' The normal reaction of a young man who was used to his girl-friend being impetuous, David thought. But could Judy be said to be impetuous? Not with himself!

Judy brought him into the room. Mrs. Venny stayed. She wasn't going to miss a thing, but for the moment she kept quiet, David noticed.

Judy said, 'Now, I want to introduce you both. This is a very dear friend, Dr. David Marland, with whose mother I'm staying. And this, David, in spite of what Mrs. Venny and everyone else has said, is my fiancé, Noel Ovenden.'

Mrs. Venny said, 'Hark at her! She's still on about it!'

The young man turned to Mrs. Venny. 'I know. You told me what happened, and I am very sorry you were put to trouble. But you won't be, any more. I'll see to it. You just leave it to me, if I may have the parlour for a bit,' and with a smile, he steered Mrs. Venny out of the room, only partly mollified, and, Judy thought angrily, quite certain to listen at the keyhole though Noel was showing her firmly the door.

He came back to them and said, 'Now!' and he shook hands with David, in a normal good-mannered way, then turned to Judy and shook his head at her. 'Oh, Judy, what am I going to do with you?' he said sadly.

'What are you talking about? They all keep saying you don't exist!' Judy exploded, but Noel's kind, head-shaking manner was making her doubtful, David noticed, with a sinking of the heart.

'You've forgotten?' Noel murmured. 'Well, I thought you wouldn't give away our little secret joke intentionally,' and turning to David, he shrugged and said, 'She is being a bit forgetful lately. Its been worrying me. The thing is . . . it's so silly, I hardly know how to explain it, sir,' thus making David feel every one of his ten years' obvious seniority, 'but you know what young couples are like, with their secret names and allusions and things? This name, Noel Ovenden, was thought up by Judy and me, when we'd been to see the film 'Dr. No' — the same initials — N-O — you see . . . ?' and he waited politely, as if David would be of too much older a generation to appreciate the wit.

David looked at Judy. She said, 'I simply don't know what you're talking about! You've always been Noel Ovenden!'

The young man glanced at David, half apologetically. 'My name's Mike Nolan,' he murmured, then turned back to Judy. 'Look, love, have you ever heard anyone else call me Mr. Ovenden, or Noel?' and she shook her head, surprised, David thought. 'Well, what *have* you heard Mrs. Venny call me?' he went on, and Judy said, almost mesmerised, 'Mr. N.' She turned to David. 'She always calls her men lodgers 'Mr.' and their initial of their surname. Not me — she doesn't like me. She gives me my full name.'

'Exactly,' the young man said, as if she had been speaking to him. 'So why didn't you expect her to call me 'Mr. O.' if you thought my name was Ovenden?

It won't wash, will it, love? Now do stop fooling about, there's a dear.'

Judy said, surprised, 'I thought it was N. for Noel,' and then looked uncertain. 'If I thought about it at all,' she finished, wavering.

'Well, so now you're back. How did the job go?' Noel said conversationally.

'What job?' Judy burst out. 'You know very well there was no job. You told me to deliver that packet and that's why I went — '

Again he glanced apologetically at David. 'What packet?' he asked.

Judy held her head. 'Oh, don't say you don't know what packet, after all I've been through! There was the most awful thing happened on the train. A nurse was thrown out and I pulled the communication cord and stopped the train and we couldn't find her and in the confusion I lost that packet you left for me to deliver. It wasn't my fault, and I've been at Dr. Marland's house recovering.'

The young man stood looking at her.

At last, he said to David, 'Perhaps you'd better go, sir. This will go on, for as long as she wants it to. It's a sort of game, you know; just for a while, then she abandons it and is quite normal. I'm used to it.'

'Didn't you send a telephone message for Miss Henderson to deliver a package to a man in Hatton Garden?' David asked bluntly, and the young man shook his head quite definitely and said, 'No. That I didn't! Why would I do a thing like that? If I had a packet to deliver, I'd do it myself, not put Judy to the trouble of going anywhere for me.' He looked down at his shoes. 'Her late employer is dead, I hear, and it may have been a bit of a shock to her. Why don't you leave her with me?'

Judy was holding her hands to her mouth, as if at any moment she would start screaming. David said, 'Yes, I think she'd better stay here tonight, but first of all, I must take your fiancée away with me, because there's something I want her to do for me,' and he smiled determinedly at both of them. His voice and manner were so normal that even Judy looked as if she were not going to start screaming after all.

Her Noel didn't like that. The flicker of his distrust was caught by David, before the bland smile took over again, and he said, 'Well, sir, she's my fiancée so you won't mind if I come along too, will you?'

David echoed the smile, with equal determination, and said, 'This, I fear, is not even for fiancés to share. It's something I want her to do for my mother, and is quite private and personal and . . . harmless. Trust your fiancée with me for an hour or two, will you?' and firmly he took Judy's arm and led her out of the house to his car.

★　★　★

Nobody came out of the house as he drove away with Judy. Nobody appeared to be watching, though Judy, he noticed, was darting anxious glances everywhere.

'I don't want to stay in that house tonight,' she said, breathlessly.

'Oh, I thought you did. I heard you say so to Mrs. Venny.'

'That was before he told all that stupid story about his name,' she said tautly. 'I'm a fool. I should have worked it out that Mr. N. didn't stand for Noel but something else. I should have thought.'

David said nothing. This was a rational approach from Judy that lightened his heart. She went on savagely, 'And now I'd like to do something else but I suppose I shall be blocked. I'd like to find out who is at the other end of the line of that number he gave he, I never did use it before so of course I never found out before last week that he wasn't there. But who is? And does he know? He probably just dug out anyone's old number to give me when I was asking for his number at his office. Probably he hasn't even got a job in an office.'

'Good girl!' David approved. 'I had already come to that conclusion myself. Smooth chap, isn't he? I hope I'm right in thinking you don't like him much now.'

'I never did like him,' she said. 'I thought I was in love with him, which is a different thing.'

'It is? Forgive an old bachelor, but I don't think I know what that means.'

'Lucky old you, Dr. Marland,' she snapped. 'All right, *David*. I'm being horrid — take no notice of me. I'm just hating everyone. I should still be in that house, screaming my head off because I couldn't stop, if it hadn't been for you, standing there so calmly, so dependable and *good*. Don't laugh. I can't quite say what I mean, but you know, some young men can be said to be charming, witty, handsome, good dancers, good with girls, very desirable all round, but not *good*. You might think I'm still raving. I hope you don't. That's the only way I can describe the way I feel about you, anyway.'

'I can't think of a nicer way to have one's self described by someone for whom one has the greatest liking and respect, Judy.'

She thought that over. 'You mean you don't think I'm going off my head?'

'I feared for your reason, yes, because I thought you'd sustained a shock. After the way you've been talking in the last ten minutes, I don't fear for you any longer,' he said firmly. 'You're okay. Hold on to that.'

'Then will you kindly tell me what's going on? You heard what he said — that he hadn't given me a packet to deliver, that he wouldn't do such a thing, that he'd heard my old employer had died and he'd been worried about me, etc., etc.,' She drew a long breath. 'You heard all that?'

'I did indeed. And I have to admit I don't know what he's up to. But if it comes to believing him or you, you are the one I'd choose to believe, somehow. Though we've a deal of explanations to find, about what's been happening to you. Now, we're in the centre of the town. Where can I park to see the solicitors?'

He couldn't, but she directed him to

someone else's private parking place that was empty and sometimes used by clients of the late Miss Remington's solicitors. He didn't like it. 'I'll get jammed in by someone and not be able to get out, or I'll get a parking ticket. No, I tell you what we'll do. Go to the house.'

'Miss Remington's house?' she gasped.

'You've still got that new key, haven't you? Well, why don't we go there and have a look round? I'd like to know what the place looks like before I see the lawyers and hear their story. Now don't say it isn't legal. It's in their interests and yours. Well, I can talk my way out of this one, I think,' he said, suddenly grinning at her and calling up an answering smile.

They drove to Highfield Avenue in silence. He wondered how she would react to the sight of the place where so much had started to happen to her, but she didn't seem unduly affected. He couldn't know that she was more put out about him and the way she was beginning to feel about him. Could such a man have so effectively, and in such a short time, almost obliterated the effect of Noel's charm and Noel's ability to make her so afraid? It was very strange. They were in Highfield Avenue before she had come to any conclusion, and to her great surprise the street of tall terraced houses seemed to have shrunk a little, and looked a little less aloof and prosperous.

The curtains of the next door house moved as usual, it was true, and those across the road, but somehow she was no longer intimidated by such things. She had David with her and he would fix everything.

But there was one thing he hadn't made allowances for and couldn't fix at all, and that was, when she got out that brand new key, she stood staring perplexed at the door. There was no place to put it in. The old key-hole was hidden by a small brass plate, and a new Yale lock had been fitted higher up.

★ ★ ★

David said, 'Well, at least it shows that the solicitors aren't as asleep as I had thought they were,' and he sounded satisfied. 'They must have had a look round when they entered with their locksmith so I don't think we need worry about the house any more.'

'Yes, we do!' she said fiercely. 'I want to show you the hole in the attic walls. You never did believe me. You don't believe me now.'

'Well, you can't show me, can you? We can't get in! What we'd better do is to go back to the solicitors and get their reactions.'

David could be very firm, so she shrugged, and agreed to walk back with him. It was only five minutes and at least they wouldn't be in trouble with the parking, in this quiet road.

At the last moment, however, when David was about to be shown in, Judy decided she didn't want to go inside. 'I'll wait here for you. It might be better if you talked with Mr. Wardlaw as man to man,' and that appealed to him. She watched David go in with a sad little smile. He would get nowhere. That old man didn't want to be told anything like that.

Once the door had closed on David, she slipped out, and walked back to the house alone. She wasn't quite sure what she wanted to do, but it was in her mind that she might possibly persuade the cleaner next door to go upstairs with her, if only to prove that their attic had no hole in the wall. Judy decided she would like to see that acidular woman's face when she really saw what was tantamount to an open entry to any burglar who happened to know about it. She walked quickly up the back lane and looked over the end fence through the branches of a small tree, at the back door of No. 15. It was opening. The cleaner was coming out. But she didn't lock the back door behind her. She slipped instead through a break in the dividing hedge between that garden and the far one and knocked smartly on the back door of that house. Judy knew there was another daily woman in charge there, while the occupants were out at work.

And she hadn't bothered to lock the back door. The temptation was too much. Judy opened the back gate and keeping in the shadow of that hedge, she slipped into the house. All was quiet, smelling of recent scrubbing, and further in, through the narrow hall which was a replica of that of No. 17, the smell of recent polishing. And beyond the closed door of the parlour the subdued tones of the two old bachelors who lived there . . .

Should she go out, knock on the front door, explain her mission to the two old men? But the cleaner might be back by then and would undoubtedly persuade them to refuse Judy permission. Of course, there might be no ladder, and she might just about get out of the house again before that woman came back.

She slipped off her shoes and ran

upstairs silently, and there, hanging from the trapdoor was a refinement Miss Remington had not had; a cord hanging, which, when pulled, obliged by lifting the trap door and bringing down its own collapsible steps. Judy ran up them, but of course, it was dark in the attic. A little light infiltrated from the landing below, when her eyes got used to the gloom, and she managed to pick out the hole in the wall. But it was a hazardous business getting across the floor to the wall. Twice she stubbed her toe with a dull thud. But she managed to crawl through, only to have to waste more time searching around to find the trapdoor to No. 17's landing. And what, she thought in dismay, was she going to use for steps down on to the landing of that house? But she had established that there was a hole in the wall, each side, for from the roof of one attic a thin sheen of light was coming down. But beyond that, there appeared to be no more holes.

It was by accident that she found the

trapdoor to Miss Remington's house and tugged it up. It fell back with a thud. It seemed a long way down to the landing, but she estimated that if she got through the hole and let herself drop, she might fall 'soft' on the fur rug below. But at that moment she heard something like laboured breathing behind her. She turned to see who was there, and felt the blow on her shoulder, and knew no more.

★　★　★

David was no longer his calm self. He had returned from a tiresome visit from the solicitors. The old man and his clerk were frankly amused at his story of the secret drawer in the base of the Buddha, the diamond necklace (Miss Remington never had such a thing in her life, they averred) and the holes in the attic walls made them roundly say 'Rubbish!' and flatly refuse to waste the firms' time on going back to the house with him to prove it. 'If it is proof you want, on behalf of the rather nervous young lady who worked for my old client, then I suggest you call in at Smith and Simpkins, the Estate Agents,' Mr. Wardlaw said expansively.

'Why would I do that?' David asked belligerently.

'Because, my dear young man, they are in process of selling No. 25, I believe, and would be no doubt glad to know that there was a hole in the attic there — but much more likely they will tell you they have inspected the attic already and will assure you that there is no such foolhardy thing as a hole.' So for Judy's sake David went to the Estate Agents, but he had to find the place, and it was clear that they had already received a telephone call from Mr. Wardlaw on the subject. They roundly said no house on their books had holes in the walls of the attic, and refused to be moved on the subject.

There wasn't much else David could do but to go back and tell Judy. She wasn't waiting in his car, as he had anticipated she would be when he found she had gone from the waiting-room. He looked for a telephone booth to call up the solicitor in case she had merely slipped out to the shops and gone back in his absence, when he saw the woman next door move the curtain. He ran up the steps.

'I believe you know the young lady who used to work for the late Miss Remington,' he began. 'Have you seen her this afternoon?'

'No, I have not, since I am hard at work all the time looking after my two gentlemen and have no time to look out of the window.'

'But you did just now,' David said pleasantly. 'And I just wondered if you had noticed when she returned to the car, and where she went. Because we should be getting back in time for my evening surgery.'

'Oh, you're a doctor, then. Well, that's as well, because it might be her what's lying in the garden of next door,' she said. 'I was just going to tell my two gentlemen there was someone lying there like, and see what they said.'

'How can I reach the garden?' he asked. 'May I come through the house?'

She was about to refuse, when the two old bachelors, hearing voices, came out of the parlour and said, 'My dear sir, of course you may! A doctor, you say you are! We didn't know the practice had changed hands — ' but David said he didn't come from this district and would explain later.

He found Judy in a bundled heap near some bushes. He looked up at the cleaner. 'Is this how she was when you saw her?' and she nodded, rather fiercely, he thought. 'And how could you see her from your window, as she was under this bush?'

'I don't know, but I did see her, and if you're going to say things like that to me, then I wish I hadn't told you and she could have been lying there forever!'

July's eyes opened at that moment. They widened when she found she was outside of the house, and that David was supporting her. 'What happened?' she gasped. 'Someone hit me in the attic. How did I get out here?'

'What's she talking about?' the cleaner demanded.

He gathered her up in his arms. 'May I bring her into your kitchen and bathe her head?' he asked, and the two elderly gentlemen said yes, of course, before their daily woman could refuse.

Judy couldn't keep quiet. 'Oh, I've got a thumping headache. You must find out who's in No. 17, David, because someone is there! At least, someone's in the attic. I was wondering how I could get down into No. 17 because the ladder wasn't there — '

'Judy, if you must talk, though I'd rather you kept quiet,' he said, as he bathed her head from warm water grudgingly procured by the daily woman, 'explain how you came to be in the garden!'

'I don't know! I came back to this road while you were in the office, and I thought I'd ask Mrs. — ' she looked blankly at the daily woman of No. 15. She had never known her name. 'Well, I thought I'd ask if they had a hole in their attic wall, but she went out and left the back door open. I know I shouldn't have gone in but it was such a temptation, and I knew she wouldn't have let me if she'd been there — '

As David told his mother when they returned to Axwood, all hell broke loose then. The old gentlemen were indignant that their daily woman should have gone out and left the place open to someone breaking in, and Judy shouted that she hadn't broken in but merely gone up, found the cord to pull down the attic steps and gone up and through the hole in the wall. The cleaner said Judy was lying and that she hadn't been out of the place and she appealed to the old gentlemen. Wasn't she there to answer their bell when they wanted more tea? Hadn't they had tea taken in such a little while before? How could the place have been left in that short time and where would she go to? Judy had said she went through the hedge, and all three of them protested that the hedge hadn't got a hole in it and that she would never go out and that the attic wasn't connected to the one next door.

'All right, show me — take me up, with your permission,' he said to the old gentlemen, 'take me up and let me see for myself!'

Permission to look in the attic was not forthcoming, on the grounds that the trapdoor was fixed, never used and hadn't been for years. Judy said shrilly, 'You'll find it open now, and the steps still down — I left them down to get back into this house!' So in face of that, they all trooped upstairs. But even David had to apologise for giving them trouble. There were no steps down and no hanging cord. The trapdoor was firmly closed, and the old gentlemen said categorically that it was fixed and they were not going to have it interfered with. 'As to a hole in the wall of the

attic, ridiculous! Whatever for?' and as
far as they were concerned, the matter
was closed, especially when the daily
woman said, 'That girl's always coming
up with some story or other and she
keeps bad company — I've seen the
men she's been with!' and that was
enough, more than enough, for the two
indignant old gentlemen.

Judy's headache didn't improve, but
she was too angry to allow anyone to
give her something for it. David had
checked that it hadn't been too severe a
blow, but he was very angry. Angry at
Judy for attempting to do something
like that on her own, to which she
furiously retorted: 'Well, would you have
done such a thing? Of course you
wouldn't! You wouldn't try anything out
that wasn't strictly correct, even if you
wanted the answer ever so badly!'

David's mother watched them both
anxiously. Useless to tell them to stop
shouting at each other, so she put in a
pertinent question of her own. 'If as
Judy seems to think, all the houses are

inter-connected, why didn't you knock at some of the doors and ask the people? I think I'd show something if someone suggested that our house was connected to the next by a hole in the attic wall!'

'I did,' David said shortly. 'At least, I knocked without success on the door of Nos. 21, 23 and 25, although I am bound to admit that the Estate Agents were probably right about No. 25. They would hardly not look into an attic, if only to see the state of the water tank, and they would soon have found a hole in the wall.'

Judy said, thinking, 'That's right. There wasn't a hole in the wall of No. 25. At least, I think it would be about that number.'

They both looked at her in surprise. 'Well, I haven't had a chance to remember it, but before I got hit from behind, I looked through the far wall and I could see light coming in from a skylight, and the wall beyond that hadn't got a hole in it. I wish I knew which house had a skylight.'

David, surprised, said, 'Oh, well, that settles it. I can tell you that. I looked particularly at the roofs when I was walking back from the solicitors. It would be the house next door to the one that's being sold.'

'So,' his mother said, 'Miss Remington's house was flanked by houses that would give an entry to hers, and one other. So you have a choice of three through which the intruder got in. What are we going to do about that?'

David, looking at Judy, said, 'Nothing, at least until the week-end, when I mean to go over to Southgrove again. Judy must rest until then.'

Judy had little fault to find with that. She was now feeling the toll of that blow, and the shock and the excitement of that day. Mrs. Marland helped her to get to bed, and said she would sleep in her room again that night.

Downstairs she and her son sat talking for a long time. 'What can it all mean?' Mrs. Marland asked him. 'It's different now, isn't it, since she's shown you that awful young man does exist, but I must say I don't feel happy about the name business. Do you really think Judy forgot they made that name up?'

'No,' David said bluntly.

'In that case, the only thing we can think of is that that young man deliberately set it up, but wasn't he taking a lot for granted? Judy might have spoken to someone else about 'Mr. Ovenden', in the house, I mean, and — '

'She probably did, at first, but I imagine he was a fast worker and got to Christian name terms. She wasn't in much and didn't talk to the other people much anyway, and she was at loggerheads with the landlady. A perfect situation, unless he was responsible for the atmosphere, too. It would have helped him. But as you say, why? *Why?*' Puzzled, he answered his own question.

'I don't know. I ask myself why he tried to suggest to me, a doctor, that she had hallucinations . . . except that he was smart enough to put it in such a way that I might construe it to mean she was teasing him, playing him up, and then coming round again. I don't know. Perhaps he didn't think I cared enough about her to do anything about it.'

There was a perceptible pause. At last, David looked up and said, 'Yes, I do, mother. I'm not one to be rushed, but I care so much that . . . I wish she could be my wife, so that I would know she was in my care completely. I'm afraid she'll take off again, and without marrying her, I can't stop her.'

'David, my dear, that's no reason for a man to get married,' she murmured.

'You don't think so, Mother? Must I tell you she's in my thoughts all the time, and that I'm worried sick when I can't actually see her, to know she's all right? Because that's how it is. In such a little while, that's how it is.'

7

'When . . . will you ask her?' his mother forced herself to ask.

'As soon as I can,' he said in a level tone. 'You don't like the idea, do you, Mother? How odd, I've never known you to go against something I wanted.' And as she didn't answer but looked so patently distressed, he said, 'You do like Judy, don't you?'

'Yes, oh yes! I more than like her! But that isn't it. To accept her into our family, to be your wife, the mother of your children . . . well, David, I am old-fashioned. I don't approve of a marriage for any other purpose. Besides, I think you have that in mind though you may not know it. David, listen to me — I'm not trying to stop you doing what you want. You're no boy. You've a career, you're much liked in the district, and I can find some-where else. It isn't that.'

'But Mother, I don't want you to go anywhere else! Bless me, you being here is half the reason I'm taking this step. You helping Judy, giving her support — without you, even marriage with me would not do the trick. I'd be away so much. Oh, don't you see?'

'I'm trying to tell you how I feel about it. We don't know anything about her. She's a sweet girl, yes, but what's wrong? You must admit something's wrong somewhere! Is it a gigantic conspiracy, and if so, why? And if it isn't, then it's her . . . her mind. David, we don't even know if it's hereditary, and it might be!' And there she broke off, afraid to go further.

She had never been afraid to talk to her son before but now he was like a stranger; a stranger fired by a deep passion for this frail looking girl who was bedevilled by strange happenings. Where would it all end?

'What do you think is the trouble, yourself?' she said at last, as he sat wrapped in that all-consuming silence.

'I don't know. I've thought and thought. And don't ask me if I've been to see my friend the sergeant, because the answer is no, I haven't had time or opportunity and if I had, I wouldn't have done. He's a good fellow but he has written Judy off as a crank; a beautiful but tiresome crank. No, he hasn't said so but I can read his thoughts. Without concrete evidence, they can do nothing.'

'But haven't we concrete evidence? Well, explanations of some odd things? And if we get explanations of those, such as the young man who wasn't supposed to exist . . . '

'Don't remind me of that, Mother. I still can't see how Judy could possibly have not heard him referred to by his real name,' he blurted out, and looked even more unhappy at that admission.

'And what about that young man? She is supposed to be engaged to him. Had you forgotten?'

'An engagement without a ring. A very loose affair. And Judy has told me she doesn't even like him.' But she had said that was different from being in love with someone, he reminded himself unhappily.

'What about those mysterious holes in the attic walls?' his mother persisted.

He looked at her as if he wished she hadn't said that. 'I believe her,' he forced himself to say, 'but I didn't see them myself, of course.'

'Well, what's a mother for but to be useful? And I'm going to be useful now. There's a way of finding out if such things exist normally. Remember that young man who came to report the Flower Show last year and stayed to try and get a job locally, because of that girl he'd got interested in? Why don't you ask him? He's still staying in the district.'

Anything. Anything to try and prove that Judy was right, his mother thought sadly, as she watched her son patiently telephoning until he tracked the young man, and then finding out something that pleased him.

His face was brighter when he turned from the telephone. 'He says it's not only possible but has been done extensively in some houses, for the purpose of a quick get-away in case of fire. He believes some houses in this town opened up their attics during the last war. Well, those in Highview Crescent are old enough for that!'

'Did he want to know why you were asking?' she put the question carefully.

David shook his head. 'No, he's full of that girl you mentioned. He was a nice chap,' he laughed. 'I suppose we couldn't bring him in on this?'

'We might, later, but I don't think I would at the moment,' his mother said, thinking. 'You see, there's still that business of the nurse on the train. We can get everything else straightened out, I believe, but never that. And until we do, well, it does smack of hallucinations, doesn't it?'

He sat down again. 'A nurse with an odd name,' he mused. 'She could have come from abroad, couldn't she, and not be listed here?'

'Whatever conclusion we come to about her name being listed or not, David, there is still no evidence to show that she was thrown out of the train. She should have been by the track somewhere, poor woman. You can't be thrown out of a train window and get up and walk away.'

'Didn't we decide that it was a bit of an act to play a trick on Judy?'

'Then that would argue those young men knew her, which she hasn't admitted. It would look worse if she did. No, she sticks to it that that girl was so very worried, and don't forget what *about* — a non-existent person at a nonexistent address in a town that is very much existing. Do you know Pillerwick?'

'No, but my friend the sergeant does, and no dice. That road isn't there.'

'So ... why did Judy listen to someone who was not telling a clearly heard story, and get involved with her? To forget a packet she was supposed to deliver and which she says was stolen from her?'

David kept walking up and down the room. 'We're being blocked; blocked at every turn, in finding out. Those solicitors were too sweeping in their assertion that there was nothing of value there. How did they know? Old people hoard things. Suppose the old lady was keeping a valuable necklace there, hidden, until she could get it out and . . . '

' . . . and what, David? It wasn't mentioned in her Will. Was it?'

'No, but her Will, so they said, embraced 'everything in the house'. Now that could have embraced a dozen diamond necklaces.'

'Yes, but it was likely that someone like Miss Remington, who didn't seem to be all that well off, would have even acquired one diamond necklace?'

'Suppose she did. Suppose someone had Willed it to her, and she kept it hidden there because she knew people were wandering about her house at night?'

'After Judy had locked up so carefully? Of that, I *can* believe Judy!'

'Can you?' he asked morosely. 'If she was so much under the thumb of that chap, isn't it just possible that she might have left something open for him?'

'David!' his mother exclaimed, shocked.

He turned a ravaged face towards her. 'It doesn't change my feelings towards Judy, but suppose she's as . . . enslaved, I suppose one might say . . . by that chap, as I . . . ' and he choked on the last words and turned away.

His mother felt she had been looking through a keyhole, or eavesdropping. Her son had never shown his feelings so nakedly before, about anything. To cover the way she felt, she said briskly, 'Well, I don't believe it. Judy's a tidy person, an honest one, I'm sure. So that leaves someone coming in from the attic, which strikes me as being much more likely. Softly entering and softly leaving, at his leisure. Ugh! What a loathsome creepy feeling one gets, at the thought! I shan't sleep tonight!'

He turned round and looked at her. 'You think he heard them talking about the necklace, and stole it, and packed it up for her to take to Hatton Garden? But how would he explain he was in possession of it, to a reputable jeweller in that street of streets? No, Mother, I do not believe one would find a 'fence' there, in spite of the thrillers you persist in reading.'

'Well, never mind poking fun at my thrillers! They have set my mind working and how is this for an idea? Never mind the necklace. Suppose someone was using No. 17 to hide *things of his own?* Things he'd stolen, perhaps. Well, if it was a mess, such as Judy describes, how would anyone know if anything had been disturbed? Or what was hidden there?'

'But what would someone want to hide there of his own? Bit of a risk, wasn't it?'

His mother sat thinking. 'I don't know. Yes, it might have been. It might just have meant the end of the old lady's life, if she . . . No, wait a bit. Suppose this chap listened in to what they were talking about? He might not necessarily have found out about the necklace, or if he had, he might not have realised its worth. No, wait a bit, what I'm thinking is, suppose he had something of value to him, not jewellery, which he wasn't supposed to have, and he'd hidden it around the place, and he'd heard Judy talking about giving the place a good turn out the next day?'

They stared at each other, appalled. 'I'd forgotten about that, until now,' his mother admitted. 'I don't suppose you even thought about it. It wouldn't matter that much to a man, unless it was a man who didn't want a big wind going through the place, such as Judy had threatened. And she'd managed to persuade the old lady to agree, if you remember! Now, it doesn't bear thinking about, but suppose someone heard that, and decided he'd have to come and collect whatever it was that he'd left in that place, perhaps in scattered hiding places? And suppose the old lady had disturbed him? Suppose he'd pushed her down the stairs?'

★ ★ ★

Inevitably the telephone rang, and their conversation was stopped, with some force. David had to run. It was a burns case; the inevitable pulling off a stove of a saucepan of hot liquid, by a child, but the adult had caught the liquid as well as the toddler. His mother watched him roar his car out of their drive and wondered how many of those casualty beds were still empty in their local hospital. That took her mind back to Judy and the way she had come to them. That nurse had fallen off the train near their town. Wouldn't you think that someone, somewhere on that train, would have seen something? She sat thinking. The odd house straddled the countryside before the town started. Suppose someone in one of those houses, had seen something? A woman cleaning an upstairs window . . . an old grandparent sitting watching the trains go by for the sake of something to see . . . She thought of the young reporter they had been talking about, but she couldn't remember his name. David would know it . . . But David wasn't the sort to agree with what she was thinking might be a good thing to do.

She sat down at the bureau by the fireplace, and wrote an experimental advertisement to insert in the Personal Column of their own paper: IF NURSE LEMIRA JEACOCK, WHO WAS TRAVELLING ON THE TRAIN FROM   TO LONDON ON THE   OF   WOULD TELEPHONE (and she inserted her own telephone number) SHE WOULD HEAR SOMETHING OF ADVANTAGE TO HER. She sat back and read it, still a little shaky at what she was doing. She would have to leave Judy to insert the times and dates, for safety's sake. She was uncertain about those. And supposing Judy didn't want to agree?

Oddly, Judy was agreeable. It was the

next day that she asked her, after David had gone on his rounds. 'What does David say about it?' Judy asked inevitably, and she had had to admit that her son didn't know about it.

'No, and you're not going to tell him, because you know he believes my story and you don't,' Judy said quietly, the antagonism back in her eyes.

'I believe you are sure you saw what you told us, my dear,' she said after a pause. 'But I defy anyone to be certain when they are being held from behind, and looking round, and only getting a glimpse of a body being hoisted to the open window by several tall young men.'

'So?' Judy said flatly.

'So I'm wondering if, presuming (as my tiresome mind will keep presuming) it was a plot which fooled an honest person like yourself, I am wondering if they were all in it together — the nurse with the convenient impediment in her speech which fluffed most of the very involved story she told you about a person nobody can trace, at a house that doesn't exist — '

'We traced Noel. He did exist, didn't he?' Judy thrust.

'That was different!' David's mother said briskly. 'At this stage I am beginning to think that that was quite unintentional, that muddle. You didn't happen to have heard his real name, and you weren't a suspicious person, and he, for reasons of his own (probably for his business, whatever it is) uses a different name. I don't know. But it has nothing to do with this business of the missing nurse.'

'Then why was she killed?'

'I don't know. I don't know that I can believe she was killed, or was even thrown out of the train window. My dear, before you interrupt, let me put this to you — could you swear on the Bible that you saw that nurse's face, her eyes, her arms and hands, as she was hoisted to the open window? And did you see all those things outside the window, as she fell to the ground?'

Judy flinched, but she thought hard, and had to admit that she wasn't sure.

'Was it a great dark thing which you immediately thought was the bulk of her navy raincoat and hat, because you were intended to think that? Don't forget, I'm an avid reader of thrillers, a fact my son is always teasing me about. I am not a fanciful person, so I suppose that's why I can't accept that this thing was done on an ordinary train, after this woman was talking to you, Judy. She must have picked you out to talk to.'

'Why would she do that? There were other people on the train! Don't ask me if they were men or women, young or old, because I don't remember, but if she was picking someone out to talk to, Why me?' She swallowed. 'Why not just anyone, who happened to be me, because she was in trouble and wanted to talk and she was sitting near me.'

'But she chose where to sit. You said yourself the train hadn't many people on it at that time of day. I'm surprised at a crowd of young men round one door if it was so empty.'

Judy stared at her, and finally, she said, 'All right.' She sat down. 'You want to get to the bottom of this, naturally you do. You don't know if I'm a criminal, come to that. If you believe it's a fishy story I've told, then you might come to believe I'm a criminal, in with the rest of the gang, whatever they were up to (if they were a gang!) and it must worry you to have me here.'

'Good gracious, that's an awful thought you've put to me! I confess I hadn't got round to thinking of that,' David's mother said. She wondered if the trend of her thoughts, towards Judy's mental state, showed in her face, as the alternative to the story of the nurse on the train being true. But Judy just stared steadily at her, so she said quietly, 'Don't say things like that to me, my dear. I like you too much to think such a thing. Besides, you'd have to be an extremely good actress, and you're not — there have been times when . . . you've shown your feelings too much to have been a good actress.'

'What feelings?' Judy asked hoarsely, a tide of red running up her face.

'The way you feel about David?' his mother prompted softly.

Judy whitened. 'And you don't like that. Of course you don't. So what are you going to do about it? You won't send this to the newspapers, I'm quite sure. David would be livid if you did!'

'It's such a pity because I think it would fetch something,' Mrs. Marland said regretfully. 'You see, if, (seen from where I'm sitting) that scene didn't happen but was an elaborate piece of acting . . . '

'But why? They didn't know me so it couldn't be a joke!'

'It was no joke, I think,' David's mother said, her thoughts jostling about so quickly in her head that she could hardly breathe for fear of losing one. She must hold on to the fragments, and make a well-knit whole! 'Look, I think, to put it bluntly, somebody wanted that packet you were to deliver. There! How does that strike you? You're a careful girl. You'd hardly be likely to give anyone a chance of stealing it from your bag, unless you were actually upset and jostled and thinking so deeply about something else (like someone being thrown from a train) that your mind would be taken off your handbag for long enough for someone to take it and close the bag again so it would be some time before you even missed it.'

'No, that won't work,' Judy said, interested in spite of herself. 'First, who would go to the length of throwing a real person out of a train — '

'Accept it, my dear, just for a minute, that it was only something that made you think it had happened!' Mrs. Marland begged. 'Well, I don't know how they did it. They might have thrown out a dark sack or something . . . no, that wouldn't do, because the track was searched. Well, I wonder if its possible for them to only pretend to throw someone out? Never mind that, the thing is, you were distracted and someone took the packet. Now, I think you believe it was this diamond necklace in it? Well, Hatton Garden, yes, it fits . . . I suppose. No, it *suggests*, and that's what everything in this whole business is . . . just suggesting things, so that one is forced to race ahead, believe them, get past to something else, and miss the fake.'

'Honestly, I don't know what you're talking about, Mrs. Marland,' Judy said, breaking in with a very worried voice. 'In the first place, I was asked by a third person to take that packet for a Mr. Noel Ovenden . . . '

'And that isn't his name!' Mrs. Marland explained. 'So it would be someone who knew of that fake name!'

'No, no, wait,' Judy said, holding her head in her hands. 'A porter gave me a note from a man he said asked him to take it to the young lady over there. That's what he said. And the note was from Noel, it was! It was like his way of speaking, all bossy, when he was in a hurry. Ring a certain number, in a line of callboxes on the station.'

'How did he know you'd be there?' Mrs. Marland pounced, excited now.

'I haven't heard that explanation yet. I did ask him but he told me to rush and get that train — that was when I was speaking to him on the telephone. And it was him, of course it was! Not just his voice, in case you're going to say someone else sounded like him, but his way of speaking. He used my name. And now — he denies any knowledge of the packet! I've just thought of that — he really did deny it!'

'When, my dear?'

'At Mrs. Venny's, when he was busy trying to make David believe I forgot things, or remembered them when it suited me. It was the first time I've ever heard that his name was Mike Nolan!' and she sounded so indignant.

'Well, I think it proves he is a liar, and probably a thief.'

Judy thought so too, which was plain from the look in her face.

'And what is more, I think he put a

fake address of Hatton Garden on the package to make it look important enough for you to agree to take it, and I don't believe he ever meant it to go as far as London. Also it was for the railway clerk to see, if he'd got inquisitive, only the man was too busy. I believe your Noel wanted that packet back, and to make people believe, when you mentioned it, that it had really been stolen. Oh, yes, and he also denied all knowledge of it too, just to make doubly sure.'

'But it's so involved!' Judy exploded.

'Of course it is,' Mrs. Marland said slowly, the seriousness of it all suddenly wiping out every vestige of excitement and the interest of playing at being a private detective. 'It's involved on purpose. But you see, I think that if that necklace is really worth thousands, and he's stolen it, the plot jolly well would have to be involved, in order to cover his own tracks, wouldn't he?'

Judy said, 'I still don't see. If he'd just taken it and quietly got away and took it to a fence or whatever people do with a stolen necklace . . . '

'Ah, yes, but that is the whole point. He might have had other people in it, people in the jewellery trade, who'd take it to pieces, melt down the settings. It would be traceable otherwise, wouldn't it?'

'Would it? Only Miss Remington and I have seen it, apparently, and Miss Remington's dead!'

And they stared at each other in horror, as the import of Judy's words clarified in their minds. Miss Remington was dead, and that only left Judy herself.

8

David's mother recovered first. 'We're being silly,' she said firmly. 'We don't know that any such thing happened. First of all, we have to remember that your old lady's death was accepted as an accident. Well, let's leave it at that. Let's consider your young man. He doesn't strike me as being a big operator. To put it bluntly, my dear, a sneak thief perhaps. One who had discovered by accident that there was that way to enter the house. For all we know, he has entered other houses with the same hole in the wall of the attic.' She looked quickly at Judy. 'What are we thinking of? We really should let the police know about this so they can check, and warn the occupants to put a bolt on the under side of the attic trap door, even if they don't want to go so far as to brick up the holes in the roof, shouldn't we?'

Judy said forlornly, 'What policeman will listen to us now? They just smile kindly when anything I say is reported.'

'Yes,' David's mother agreed. 'Which is either a lucky accident for your young man, or . . . and here we go again, back to the thought of a big gang set-up . . . they reckoned on that effect. And if that's the case, they could have set up the business on the train. And why?'

The daily woman came and Mrs. Marland left Judy, with the insistence that she didn't go out without telling her. Judy nodded vaguely and sat staring as if mesmerised, into the single bar of the electric fire, which had been put on against the sharpness of the day. Warn people, about those holes. How would it be if someone knocked and asked to buy things in the attic? Good prices given. Anything to make the owners go up and look into their attics . . .

She pictured herself going to Highview Crescent to do this chore, because who else would? It became an important thing to do, if only to be able to say to the police: now, I have proved I'm right about those holes, so the other things I've said must be taken as true! The idea caught hold of Judy until she felt smothered in the house and went to find Mrs. Marland to tell her.

There was only the daily woman, standing at the back door with the baker. 'Oh, it's you, miss! I'm glad there's someone in to settle this because it's not my business to pay bakers,' she said with a sniff. 'She's gone out!' she added.

'Oh. Did she take the car?' Judy asked, her last hope going, and the woman nodded, and went back to her cleaning.

'Look, I don't know anything about the account, but — '

'It's not the account, it's how many muffins for tea,' the baker grinned.

'Oh. Well, a dozen, I suppose, if that's usual,' and she watched him go out to his van. From where she stood, she could see someone else. The man in the zippered jacket, stopping to light a cigarette.

When the baker came back, Judy had

snatched up her coat and bag and was tying a square round her head. 'Would you do something for me? I promised I'd stay in but I've remembered the Post Office. I suppose you wouldn't give me a lift to the end of the road, so I can dash?'

'On telephone duty?' he grinned. 'Okay. Hop in the cabin,' and he went next door. The last house of delivery in their road.

Judy scrabbled in her handbag and found her sun glasses. The day was bright enough for them, though very cold. She pulled up her collar and huddled down to wait, and the man in the zippered jacket appeared to have noticed nothing. Even when the baker came back and drove away, Judy saw in the mirror the man hadn't moved. She breathed again. Then she remembered — this was a Southgrove firm. 'I suppose you couldn't let me stay here all the way to Southgrove?'

'I'd do that for anyone who'd been told to stay indoors a day like this!' he said, laughing, and proceeded to bore her all the way with details of the greenhouse he was building. She persuaded him to drop her at the Southgrove Post Office and from there she walked to Highview Crescent, and nobody appeared in the least interested in her.

Now she had money in her purse she felt better. She felt better still having caught at least two occupants at home at that time of day and had the satisfaction of being given an old hockey stick, a bag of elderly garments she swore would do fine for the church dramatic society's box and some back numbers of a glossy magazine. She said innocently, 'These seem dry. I don't suppose your attic would have a hole in the wall to the next house? Well, I heard the other day that some of these houses were interconnected.'

The woman's face cleared. 'Oh, is that it? It gave me quite a turn when I saw it! I've never been up there before. My husband usually opens the trap and throws things in. Oh, but it's nasty. I'll get him to have it bricked up.'

Judy went away very happy, especially as the next house owner wouldn't admit to such a thing (clearly under the impression that to give such information to a stranger would be to invite burglars) but the shock on her face was there. She hadn't known about the hole. She was too upset to offer anything at Judy's request. This, too, might well have been the house with the attic that had looked empty in the gloom when she herself had looked through. She checked the number.

No. 21 and No. 19 had a hole in the attic wall. She hugged herself as she boarded a bus and went on top. She had money for fares and adored a top front seat. But the joy went out of her ride when another passenger came up and sat in the other double front seat, and like herself, took a ticket back to Axwood. The man in the zippered coat.

He took no notice of her, and looked vaguely out of the bus windows as if he had nothing in the world of interest to do. But her heart banged uneasily. She *was* being followed! How could there be any doubt about it?

Shake him off, that was what she must do. So she tried. She got off the bus at a stop further on than David's road, and had to walk back, and for good measure she went into the church and sat down for a while. But the man was there, examining the notices in the porch when she emerged. She ran, and although he didn't appear to do anything so undignified himself, he was there outside of the house when she had removed her coat and gone to peer through a chink in the curtains. He was there, and he knew where she was . . .

David's mother was put out because she had gone out after all. Judy could only mutely point to the man across the road.

'But that's David's patient, dear. He's only waiting for the surgery to open. Didn't you hear David say he expected to see him tonight?'

Judy said, 'Probably. Very likely. But that doesn't explain how he happened to be on the bus from Southgrove, does it? Beside me?' and she told David's mother where she had been and why.

'My dear, what a risk to take! I do wish you wouldn't! If you'd said, I would have come with you. We could both have been collecting for the Jumble Sale.' But she was pleased with the result, Judy could see.

The sat down to tea and toasted muffins by the fire, and Judy said she'd like to look at the old magazines before they got given away. The hockey stick and the clothes were stowed away with Mrs. Marland's collection for the Jumble sale. All was peace until David came in.

His eyes went straight to Judy, and though he said only a few common-places, his mother felt that he had forgotten her presence and was saying sweet personal things to that frail girl who was determined to clear her own name. Mrs. Marland went out to make fresh tea, and forgot to put tea in the boiling water, she was so fussed.

She must tell David about the man Judy thought had been following her. All very fine to pretend he was just a patient, but to be on the same bus from Southgrove was too much of a coincidence, especially as she herself had noticed him in their road when she had gone out earlier.

Surgery that night was a full one. She said she would help David on every other night, so that Judy wouldn't be too tired, and they left Judy listening to the radio. Judy said she'd take any telephone calls to help them, so neither of them took much notice when the telephone began to ring soon afterwards.

Judy answered it, and her heart turned over. It was Noel. 'Long time no see,' he said mockingly. 'What happened to your intention to come back to Mrs. Venny's?' So Judy had to think up something quickly.

'I wasn't feeling too good and Dr.

Marland insisted on my going home to bed. That's what comes of living in a doctor's house.'

'Oh, I see,' Noel said and appeared quite satisfied. 'Still, you *are* intending to come back soon, I suppose? There's some reason for saying that, Judy.'

'What?' she asked guardedly.

'There's a way to speak to your fiancé,' he said, sounding genuinely hurt. 'Especially when he's bought the ring, at long last. What's the stunned silence for? I said I would when I had enough cash, and I have got enough and I have bought a ring. A neat diamond, not flashy, to interest madam,' he said, a laugh in his voice. Noel at his most charming and insidious.

'I wish you hadn't, Noel. I mean, I'm having second thoughts. Well, I've had such a rotten time that I'm not sure I want to get married or even be officially engaged. And what's that got to do with my coming back to my room?'

'Oh, that,' he sighed. 'It's only my feeling, of course, but I get the odd sensation that the old girl's intending to quietly let your room to someone else at the same time as she's hanging on to the rent you gave her. Of course, you may not mind some stranger being in your room, where all your things are . . .'

'Oh, Noel! She can't do that, can she?' Judy cried.

'She couldn't if you slipped back here for the odd night. Catch her on the hop, so to speak. Then she wouldn't dare do it, never knowing when you were going to turn up, if you see what I mean.'

'Well, I might have to do that,' she said worriedly.

'I'll pick you up in half an hour,' he said, and rang off before she could say no.

She was shaking all over again. It wasn't like her to be scared, she told herself fiercely. Why couldn't she just say no to Noel, on the doorstep? Dr. Marland was here. He wouldn't let Noel over-ride her if she didn't want to go back with him! But at the same time . . .

She had almost made up her mind to brave Noel's invitation and to go with him, even if she didn't actually stay the night in her room at Mrs. Venny's. After all, she could make the excuse that she had come to change into her one long dress which was still hanging up in the wardrobe there, couldn't she? And then Judy remembered the man in the zippered jacket who had been tailing her today. He would have told Noel she had been to the doors of the houses near No. 17. and that was why Noel was inviting her out. He would want to know why. He would get the information from her.

When the doorbell rang, she didn't answer it. She put the light out and peeped through the side window. There was somebody there, but no car at the kerb. Supposing it was a new patient, who didn't know where the surgery door was? Indecisive, she let the doorbell ring again. Mrs. Marland called, 'Judy, be a dear and answer that, will you? We're tied up here.' So she had to go.

The hall light was out. She wished she had left the light on in the sitting-room. At the last moment she put the chain on the door. The bell rang again, more imperiously this time. She rushed back and put the sitting-room light on, so that enough light would trickle out without letting Noel see how afraid she was. Coward, coward, she told herself, and opened the door.

It only allowed two inches of space, with the chain on. Judy looked through at the person standing there. Not Noel, but someone who struck far more fear into her. She heard her own choking cry, smothered in her throat, as the person whispered, '*Let me in! Let me in!*'

The scream that rose to Judy's throat was still-born, yet must have made some sort of cry, for Mrs. Marland hurried out of the surgery. The light slanted out on Judy, sheet-white, slipping into a heap on the floor, her back against the door, which shut it. Judy was glad it had shut it, shutting out that untidy grizzled hair, the wild wide eyes, the terrible whispering demand, and as consiousness left her, she heard her own voice, as from a long way, murmuring, 'Miss Remington came back . . . she wanted to come in . . . '

★   ★   ★

David lifted Judy up and carried her into the now empty surgery. That had been the last patient. He lay her down and said to his mother, 'Look after her — I must go and see who it was.'

'No, don't go, David!' she said.

'You, too? Don't let Judy scare you. It must have been old Mrs. Jones. She will do these things,' and he was gone. She could hear his footsteps pounding down the path. As she bathed Judy's face, she reflected that David would of course want to prove at once that it had been a person, to face Judy with the truth when she came to. Otherwise they would never be able to eradicate the conviction that a ghost had been clamouring for admittance, incredible though it seemed that someone as rational as Judy could think that.

Again Mrs. Marland was not sure. She thought of people who brainwashed others to think things. She thought of the drugs that could be given, to induce such a condition. But Judy had continually insisted she had been given nothing, and she herself knew, from helping Judy undress, that first day in this house, that the tell-tale needle spots were not in evidence anywhere.

David, who had gone out in his white coat, would be cold, she reflected. It was a frosty night, thick on the path. With a checked exclaimation she rushed out and look down, with the light of the hall pointing a long bright slant on the outside path. There were two sets of prints in the frosty surface of the path. She could almost have cried for joy.

As she was returning to the hall, David was coming along, with another person. A woman, but she had a great scarf all over her head and face and she was walking with a curious bent stride, a manish stride with the bent shoulders of an old woman. In spite of herself, Mrs. Marland felt a little apprehensive. What Judy could do, to scare people, she tried to laugh at herself.

David signalled to her, and she construed it to mean to put the light out, so she did, and with his arm under the person's elbow, they slid quietly in.

'Judy?' he asked in a hushed tone.

His mother nodded towards the surgery. She could still see Judy's feet, on the end of the couch. She was still unconscious.

'Good,' David said. 'Go to her, and see if you can get her to bed when she comes to. We'll go in here, in the warm, and remember, Mother, I don't want Judy to . . . ' and he broke off as the person with him nodded vigorous agreement.

Judy came to soon after that. She looked very ill. Mrs. Marland said, 'Silly girl, whatever did you think you saw on our front doorstep?'

Judy said, 'Miss Remington.'

'She's dead, my dear,' David's mother said quietly but firmly. 'It was someone else. And if you're going to live in a doctor's house you must get used to odd people doing rather odd things. Now, do you think you can manage to walk upstairs to bed if I help you? You must have an early night and get some sleep.'

'I haven't told you yet . . . ' She made an effort and told Mrs. Marland about Noel's telephone call.

'Oh, my dear, why didn't you come and tell me?'

'What, in surgery? With a patient there?' Judy protested.

Mrs. Marland said, 'Better keep away from the telephone for a bit,' and she helped the girl upstairs, put the electric fire on in her room, and gave her a hot water bottle. She started to shuffle the old magazines away into a corner cupboard, but Judy said, 'I don't feel sleepy. Perhaps I could read a bit. Take my mind off everything. Do you think?'

So David's mother left them on the table by the bed.

Down in the sitting-room, she found David sitting, his white coat now removed, talking quietly to a very odd-looking woman. No wonder Judy, after encountering Noel on the telephone, had been disturbed by this apparition. The woman had the oddest clothes on — those of someone considerably older than herself — and her hair hadn't been combed for ages, Mrs. Marland thought fastidiously. But David said, 'Brace up, Mother — guess who this is?' and as she shook her head in bewilderment, David said, with a funny little smile, 'Miss Frances Banford — the missing niece of the late Miss Remington.'

His mother's legs gave way and she flopped into a chair, belatedly remembering to extend a hand to say 'How do you do?'

Her own hand was crushed in a hearty grip which surprised her, especially as the answer came in an indecipherable whisper.

'No wonder Judy was shocked,' David said. 'Miss Banford tells me she is wearing some of her aunt's clothes.'

'But why?' his mother asked blankly, with a great want of manners.

'Oh, there's a reason,' he said quickly. 'First of all, Miss Banford's lost her voice, which explains why she whispered, and as she was in a hurry, 'Let me in' seemed the most direct thing to say. She didn't mean to scare Judy.'

'Well, she did!' his mother protested.

'Mother, would you go and shut up the surgery door, please? We don't want any more people coming in. Then come back here. This is important.'

'I have done it, David,' his mother said shortly. 'After Judy passed out, I shot round and shut up everywhere. I'm getting as worried as that poor child is.'

'Well, that's as well,' he said. 'Now, Miss Banford tells me she's got a problem.'

'The solicitors have too, I gather,' Mrs. Marland said. 'Does she know they're searching half the world for her before Probate can be taken out?'

'Mother, Miss Banford isn't deaf. She's just lost her voice. Shall I tell my mother, to save you straining your throat?' he suggested, and when his visitor nodded vigorously, he said, 'Miss Banford was trying to hail a taxi and keep hidden at the same time, round the corner. Not a very easy thing to do. She saw a chap across the road — '

'Oh, dear, David, not your patient, with the zippered jacket?'

'Yes, but Mother, he's employed by her to look after Judy. He's a private enquiry agent,' David explained, but he didn't look any less worried. 'But he warned her, as she walked past him, that there was some other chap doing the same job, for the other side, presumably. So that's why she wanted to get in quickly and talk to Judy. She would have telephoned to ask in the normal way but lost her voice abroad and has come back sooner than she intended, to try and find a specialist to help her. Otherwise, she'd still be in the Middle East.'

'Oh, and you have heard about your Aunt's death from the solicitors?'

'No,' David broke in. 'She told me about that. She went straight to her aunt's house, just before the lock was changed and let herself in.'

'Oh! Oh, I see!' and then Mrs. Marland began to get really interested.

Frances Banford had never been really close to her aunt. Her interests were sight-seeing in a starkly simple way, usually alone, with the purpose of writing a book. She was tough, healthy, very upset at losing her voice, and rather quick to catch on to certain things that hadn't seemed right. She had heard someone moving about furtively, and hidden behind one of Miss Remington's heavy, dusty old curtains, and seen a young man feverishly searching the place.

'The description rather fits our Noel Ovenden,' David said.

He hadn't been searching in drawers and cupboards, but in such odd places as picture rails, under the base of a tall wooden clock case on the mantelpiece, and on the bottoms of armchairs. 'Anywhere where a person might tape something into place at the base of a thing, where it wouldn't be examined.' But apparently his search had been in vain. Finally he ran up the stairs and didn't come down again. Miss Banford, curious and not at all afraid, went quietly up the stairs, until she reached the loft, where she heard someone moving about and then there was silence. Dust was on the surface of the floor below the trap. Miss Banford found the step ladder and went up, to find that two or three other houses were inter-connected.'

'And did she tell the solicitors this?' Mrs. Marland asked blankly.

'No, because of her voice,' David said patiently. 'You haven't met old Wardlaw. He's the last person you'd want to tangle with, without a voice. Bad enough to talk with him, with a strong voice like mine!'

'So nobody knows Miss Banford is in this country?' his mother asked.

'Not sure of that,' Miss Banford whispered and left David to explain.

'She went to see her aunt's doctor, expecting to hear she'd been admitted to hospital. But the housekeeper said he'd gone away for a bit. Without disclosing who she was, Miss Banford asked whose voice was shouting. The housekeeper is deaf, as you know, but finally by writing down a few things, she elicited the information that it was a horrible black bird in a cage that the doctor was looking after for a dead patient, and the housekeeper said she was glad she couldn't hear it for the doctor complained enough about the noise it made.'

'A dead patient? Oh, I see. So that's how you knew about your aunt,' Mrs. Marland said sympathetically.

David broke in on these pleasantries. 'Never mind that, mother. The thing was, the wretched bird was shouting, 'Get Judy! Send for Judy!'.'

Miss Banford whispered, 'Very intelligent bird though not everyone's choice of a pet. I asked to see it but of course she wasn't in a very hospitable mood.'

David shrugged. 'Pity, that. Did the bird know you, Miss Banford?'

She nodded quickly. 'My aunt thought a lot of it.'

Mrs. Marland said, 'Why should the bird ask for Judy? I have never heard Judy express any particular liking for it though she was very worried about the two old cats and the poor little Peke. That died, you know. At least . . . '

'Exactly!' Miss Banford whispered, nodding vigorously again.

'Miss Banford feels there's something extremely odd going on, because the solicitor's clerk has been there. Miss Banford had been sleeping in the place.'

'For how long?' Mrs. Marland asked.

'Two nights,' David grinned. 'But she never overheard anything discussed because there was never more than the one person there at a time, and he searched with the aid of a torch.'

'How was it she wasn't seen?' Mrs. Marland gasped.

David was appreciating this very much.

He smiled broadly. 'Miss Banford has been a white hunter. She knows how to hide and how to keep dead still.'

'And she told you all this while I've been upstairs with Judy?'

'No. I know a lot of it, from what I've heard from a mutual friend of ours. Another traveller, that I was at school with. Only I didn't know she was related to Judy's Miss Remington.'

Mrs. Marland said she'd better provide a meal, but when she was going to uncomfortably suggest that their unexpected guest should stay the night, David forestalled her by saying Miss Banford wanted to go back to Highview Crescent.

'Will she be safe there, David?'

'Oh, mother, don't be so silly — a person like Miss Banford doesn't worry about hazards in Highview Crescent after the jungle and the desert.'

But Mrs. Marland felt that David and Miss Banford didn't know the half of it, though she couldn't have said what she meant by that.

'Why did Miss Banford employ a private detective to look after Judy?' she did ask, not really expecting the answer she got.

'They have hidden something in No. 17. They've got to find it before Miss Remington's niece is officially brought home by the solicitors, and inherits all her aunt left. *She* can't personally protect Judy so she provided someone. Well, Mother, Miss Remington is not here, but Judy is, and they might decide they want to question her about what they lost.'

'What would it be?' she whispered, thinking about the diamond necklace. She turned on Miss Banford, rather fiercely, David thought. 'Do you realise what that poor girl has been through? Things have happened to her that nobody can believe. But one thing I do know — they won't find it there because that Noel sent it away. He gave it to Judy to deliver and she was robbed of it on the train.'

David looked oddly at her. 'Miss Banford said the idea of a diamond necklace is simply not on. Her aunt never had that sort of money. The only stuff that will fetch anything in that house is the stuff she's brought back herself for her aunt.'

'So she would know about the secret drawer in the Buddha?'

Miss Banford whispered something and David had to get very near to hear it. Her voice had almost completely gone. David looked up and said, 'It would seem that that is another of our Judy's more fanciful stories. I must say I didn't think it very likely myself that a Buddha would have a secret drawer in it.'

He thought his mother was going to break down, she looked so wretched. 'I believe Judy,' she said fiercely. 'Anyway, if they're not looking for a necklace, what *are* they looking for?'

'Drugs, she thinks,' he said quietly.

David's mother was alarmed again. 'Oh, David, and you a doctor!' She thought, and said, 'Oh, she'll want you to go too and identify the drugs if they're found.

David, don't get involved!'

'We are involved, dear,' he said gently. 'You, me, Judy, Miss Banford here. And while we're on about the subject, don't you think she can recognise any drug, after all she's seen on her travels?' and Miss Banford nodded, with raised eyebrows and a wry smile, and spread her hands.

She got up to go. 'I'll drive her over to Southgrove,' David said, but Miss Banford shook her head. 'Back door?' she whispered. 'Take a bus. Better.'

She didn't ask to see Judy. Perhaps she had got too tired trying to communicate with that vanished voice. She moved with a slinky step which must have alarmed Judy. A hush-hushing sound, from long skirts and soft soles. Mrs. Marland watched her being shown out by David. Of course, if the woman kept her face hidden with that scarf thing, she would look no more odd than half the passengers on the buses in the district, with their odd 'Granny' clothes and long untidy hair.

But the thought of that woman, living alone in No. 17. while people were searching, made her flesh creep. Someone would get a shock.

'Well, now you can tell your friend the sergeant,' Mrs. Marland said angrily, when David came back. 'Poor Judy, and all she's had to suffer!'

'I cannot tell my friend the sergeant anything, until we have proof,' David said quietly. 'Miss Banford wants the run of that house until she finds herself what they are looking for. Then we can move.'

'How do you know it *is* Miss Banford?' his mother asked, scandalised. 'Did she show you any credentials? It might be someone from the other side, coming here to find out how much we know!'

'Considering she's done all the talking, mother,' David laughed. 'And considering she let me look at her throat and it does seem to show signs of what I think it will turn out to be, and which a friend of mine in London might well be interested in, when he returns from Switzerland,' and he took her face and tilted it. 'Poor darling, you are having a rough time since I met Judy,' and he he said the name 'Judy' as though it were part of a poem or a song.

'And another thing,' she said fiercely, 'Why is she wearing Miss Remington's clothes?' She swallowed as another thought struck her. 'How do we know if a word she uttered is true? I've got another solution. It's an actress, made to look like Miss Remington, in her clothes and everything, to give Judy a shock and make her scream out that it was a ghost. Everything to discredit Judy and make people think she's losing her reason! And you fell for it too, David! How could you?'

Now she had him worried, too. His mother continued, 'All that stuff about her remaining hidden in the house while they searched, and didn't find her! Is that likely?'

'No, I confess I was doubtful there. On the other hand, is it likely that someone from their own side would tell us about them going in to search, and suggesting they were drug-runners?'

'Judy! I forgot! She's sitting up in bed looking at magazines. Do you think she heard any of that?' Mrs. Marland asked, running to the foot of the stairs and listening. There was no sound up there, even when she called softly, but an odd sound came from the kitchen.

With David near her, Mrs. Marland crept out there and gently pushed the door open, to find Judy trying to stoke the boiler and burn something.

It was one of the old magazines she had been looking at. They took it away from her and shut the stove up, and Judy collapsed on a chair and burst into tears. 'Why, why?' she sobbed. 'Why did she do it? I trusted her so!'

'Who, love?' David asked, gathering her up in his arms, and pushing her hair back. Her face was crumpled like a child's. 'Miss Remington! No wonder she came here tonight to warn me. Don't say it wasn't her ghost — it must have been.'

'Darling girl, it was her niece. Hence the likeness,' David said. 'Now what is it you think you've seen in that tatty old magazine?'

'Oh, I can see, I think,' Mrs. Marland said, and held it out for him to look at a colour plate of a necklace. Dripping with diamonds, with a huge glistening pendant hanging at the base. 'The Frabham Diamonds, stolen from Frabham Manor several months ago', the account began, and gave a run-down of those and other jewels never recovered from a spectacular robbery at that country house. 'Was this the necklace in the drawer in the base of the Buddha, Judy?'

Judy nodded.

'But Miss Banford said the Buddha hadn't got a drawer, and couldn't have one,' David said.

'It wasn't Miss Banford. It couldn't have been,' Judy said dully. 'I remember hearing what the solicitor and the doctor were saying, that day, the last day I was in the house. Talking about them both, they were. Miss Remington and her niece.

I can't remember just what they said, only I got the impression that there was no likeness there at all, and no liking for each other, either.'

9

There was a stunned silence. The clock ticked with sinister rhythm on the mantlepiece and the sound of a car revving up was too loud. David was the first to speak and he said, 'What a lot of rot! Of course it's Miss Banford. Now look, Judy, my love, you've got to shake yourself out of all this. Look, take her up to bed, mother. Tuck her in and we'll go up and talk to her about what we've been saying. With a bit of luck we can talk her to sleep,' he muttered.

Judy refused to go up. 'Let me sit in the sitting-room. I fancy I can hear things tapping on the window. I think — I really think I'm going out of my mind.'

'No, that's what they want you to think!' David said.

They turned up the other bar of the electric fire and pulled the dark curtains. The sitting-room could be very cosy on a cold night. In her fluffy dressing-gown, borrowed from his mother, Judy looked too young, with dark smudges under her eyes; her eyes were too large for that thin face. She did look ill. He pushed the thought away from him and said, 'Now listen. This is how it is as I see it, and I don't mind saying I think its a perfect godsend that that poor woman came here tonight, and clarified my mind on several points.'

Judy shook her head slowly, but he ignored it, and went over everything from the beginning, as he saw it. 'You got hold of the wrong name for this chap, and I am convinced he laid the thing on; made you get the impression that was his name. I don't believe there was any joke about a film you both saw.'

He waited for Judy to deny this but she didn't. She just sat looking at him, waiting, it seemed to him, for him to really talk her out of all she was beginning to believe. So, knowing what rested on all this, from Judy's point of view, he did his best.

'He wanted you to get the old lady's signature and you didn't want to but it fell through because of something that happened at the house. We don't know whether the old lady had an accident and fell, or had a heart attack, or in fact was frightened to death by the sight of that young man prowling about in the dark. The chances are she was frightened to death, especially if she had seen him searching, as her niece tells me she saw him.'

'Searching? She said that?' Judy could hardly believe it, having fixed it in her mind that that was an actress, and was with the other side. The enemy.

'She has seen enough on her travels to guess he was looking for drugs. He had probably stashed away small packs of the stuff. He searched, she said, in odd corners, such as on the picture rails, under chair seats — anywhere, in fact, where an energetic young woman like yourself, bent on going through the house on a spring-cleaning jaunt, might discover them by accident.'

'Drugs?' she whispered. '*Noel*?'

'Well, perhaps he didn't hide them himself. Perhaps he knew of people who had been hiding them. Overheard them, if he snooped everywhere like he knew of people who had been hiding them. Overheard them, if he snooped everywhere like he snooped at No. 17. In which case, if he could get at them first, he could claim a reward for them, either from the police or the owners, and there would be very big money in it for him. Or he could have hidden them himself and was trying to find them to gather them in but . . . now who would have found them, got at them first, because Miss Banford said he seemed to find nothing and grew more angry with every minute.' An awful thought occurred to him. 'Judy, you didn't . . . ?'

'Gather them in?' she asked, licking dry lips. 'No, I left them where they were. I didn't know they contained drugs. I thought they were powder medicines Miss Remington took, and had hidden — well, she was queer like that. If she didn't want to see a thing around, she put it in a place that she'd forget. She once said if she had to take medicine, she'd die first. She hated illness.'

David looked drawn with anxiety, on Judy's behalf, and his mother could see why. 'Judy, I don't want to scare you, but I don't want you to go out of this house alone any more. Do you understand? I must see my friend the sergeant about this.'

Judy smiled mirthlessly. 'He won't believe you. Just another story from that crazy girl your mother has got staying with her, that's what he'll say!'

'But something must be done!' he fretted. 'I'll go and talk to him anyway. I'll tell him everything. Now the old lady's niece is in this country we ought to be able to get something done. I wonder when she'll tell the solicitors she's home? Well, I can understand her not wanting anyone to know, since she's accidentally discovered that very odd things are going on.'

He looked at Judy. 'Did you hear

anything of what had been happening as you passed this open door?' and as she shook her head, he went over everything again with her. 'So you see, the chap in the zip jacket is really looking after you, so you don't have to worry about him. But the other chap who was hanging about . . . that's another matter.'

Judy said suddenly, 'I know that a lot of men wear zippered jackets. But it was the way he walks that made me keep recognising him. And anyway, don't private detectives wear things you'd never remember? And not make themselves conspicuous?'

David said, 'Well, you might say that for the other side, too. They seem to have been making themselves conspicuous, anyway. And if you're going to insist that the zippered jacket chap was the enemy, no, I really don't think they'd be so stupid, my dear.'

'What was wrong with his hand? How did it happen?' Judy asked suddenly.

'It looked like a knife wound and that

was what it turned out to be, only not quite the way I thought of it. Not in a fight, you see, but cutting the string of a parcel — the knife slipped.'

Judy continued to stare at him, as if she simply didn't believe it. 'Why should Miss Banford have gone to the expense of employing someone to look after me, especially as she realised I was staying in the house of friends?'

'Well, she's not an ordinary sort of person. She has her own methods. Come to think of it,' David said, 'I might employ someone to watch over you if I'd discovered that drug trafficking was involved, and no evidence to offer the police.'

'Why didn't she write and tell the solicitors she'd lost her voice and was coming home? Why didn't she write and tell her aunt? I know she didn't. I saw every letter that came into that house.' Judy had her unfriendly look on again, David's mother noticed. She didn't like David believing that that woman really was Frances Banford.

David's mother felt anxious, a little scared again — but David had looked at the woman's throat, hadn't he? He hadn't liked the look of it. Judy switched her glance to David's mother, and said, 'Do you believe she's Frances Banford as well? Do you?'

'I haven't any reason to believe otherwise, my dear. Yes, I think I do, because if she was on the other side she wouldn't have mentioned drugs, would she?'

'If she's on the other side, she knows you are both dear kind people who take a person's word. She now knows what the inside of this house looks like and that I am staying here. She needn't have scared me like that. She could have just knocked and waited to be let in. And why is she wearing old clothes of Miss Remington's? Instead of her own practical, rather mannish clothes.'

'But how did you know about her, Judy?'

Judy shrugged. 'The doctor was talking about her to the solicitor, remember? In such a few well-chosen words, I got a picture of Frances Banford. Those two men don't like women who travel the world alone and wear masculine clothes and I gather she had a strong masculine voice.' She stared straight ahead.

David's mother said, 'Poor thing, how inhibited she must feel with no voice at all, then, especially if she's the sort who likes to get things done quickly and efficiently. And I suppose when you come to think of it, Miss Remington's clothes are as good a disguise as any other, in case anyone else got the impression you got, in such a little while, my dear.'

'Impressions,' David muttered worriedly, and turned away. 'I suppose I should really have asked for some sort of identity but it looked damned churlish, come to think of it. She offered information so willingly.'

'Judy,' his mother asked suddenly, 'why didn't you ask Miss Remington just what those little packets were that you kept finding?'

Judy seemed far away in her thoughts. David's mother had to repeat what she had said. The girl finally admitted, 'There was so much on my mind. Noel badgering me, and trying to persuade Miss Remington to let me clean the house out.'

'But why? I can't understand why you wanted to take on such a job!'

'It was all so dirty,' Judy admitted. 'I liked her but I didn't like her way of accumulating rubbish. It all smelt so musty and dusty. Besides, it would have been an interesting job instead of having to waste so much time finding old letters that had to be answered. I don't know, I thought at the time it would be a good thing. I wish I hadn't suggested it now.'

David's mother met her son's eyes with something like agony. David thought, in alarm, good heavens, surely she doesn't think Miss Remington was really a receiver, under the guise of a nice old lady? 'I don't think Miss

Remington could have had any idea that those packets were around,' he said quickly, to appease his mother, lift her anxiety. But then it raised another point. Wouldn't Judy have been acting more naturally if, on finding the little packets, she had taken them straight to her employer and asked what they were? Or had she really guessed and suspected Noel? The whole thing was becoming more of a tangle. 'It won't do,' he said suddenly. 'Judy's been here almost two weeks and I've been thinking. We keep holding to the thought that there is a gang of criminals making a set-up to lead her (or other people) to think she talks a lot of nonsense, but never once have they tried to contact her.'

Judy looked quickly at him. Now she was suspecting people, for that remark of his had ended on an upturned note, making it almost a question. 'Perhaps Noel will answer that question for us,' she said softly. 'He did say he would pick me up in half an hour. It's a long half an hour, isn't it?'

'Well, you're not going!' David was scandalised. 'You go back to bed, Judy!'

'All right,' she said meekly, and went. David said to his mother, 'I'm so worried, I think I will go and have a talk with my friend, the sergeant.'

'But he's gone off duty,' his mother reminded him.

'Yes, I know. I thought I'd pop round to his house. You can get me on his telephone number there, if you want me,' and he wrote it down. 'Let's pray no one will want an emergency visit while I'm talking to him. I just must hold his attention while I tell him all this.'

It was quiet after David had gone out. His mother sat thinking about everything, and felt so dejected that she turned the television on. Judy's room was not on this side of the house so it wouldn't disturb her. So she didn't know that Judy's meek acquiescence hadn't really meant she had intended to go to bed. The girl had gone straight upstairs and got dressed, in warm street clothes, and stood at the window in the darkened room, waiting for Noel to come.

His car had nothing spectacular about it so Judy watched very closely and in keeping her eyes open for a car, almost missed Miss Banford. Still in those awful clothes, she had come quietly up the path, just as she had done before. But she didn't ring the bell. She made no sign at all, that she was there, waiting to be admitted. Perhaps she was having second thoughts about bothering the Marlands again tonight. Or dropped a note in.

Judy couldn't bear it. She went softly downstairs and let herself out, closing the door quietly behind her. Miss Banford had gone back to the street and was waiting to cross the road. She was behaving as if she hadn't realised Judy was following her. There had been no note on the mat, so what had the woman wanted? Everything screamed in Judy's head to go back to that house and safety.

Half of her wanted to believe this was Miss Banford, but half of her kept remembering the doctor saying there was no likeness between the two women. And wasn't it very queer that Miss Banford hadn't written to either the doctor, the solicitor or her aunt, to announce her impending return to this country, especially as she had no voice with which to make explanations on her arrival?

Noel was sitting in his car at the end of the road. He called softly to Judy, and hearing his call, Miss Banford, on the other side of the road, stopped. Noel said, 'Get in, Judy! Let's not wait here all night!' and he held open the door for her, with that air of confidence that almost mesmerised her into getting in. Useless to say, 'But I wanted to speak to Miss Banford!' because Miss Banford had crossed the road and was standing beside her.

Noel said, 'And what are *you* waiting for? Get in, for heaven's sake, before our friend the doctor decides to return in a hurry and mess everything up.' So

Miss Banford tipped the front seat forward, pushed Judy in the back and got in beside her. Noel's car smoothly moved away from the kerb and he drove out of Axwood and took the Southgrove road.

Judy said, 'Noel, I haven't told them I'm going to be out long,' but he merely laughed. 'You don't understand! They're worried about me!'

'I bet they are!' and he laughed for some minutes, as though he knew of a lot more amusing things than he felt he could tell her. Judy was much more interested in Miss Banford, who was laughing as loudly as Noel.

'I thought you'd lost your voice!' Judy said in surprise.

'Did you indeed,' 'Miss Banford' said, in a tone of voice that reminded Judy of some other voice she had heard. 'Considering your friend is a doctor, he is really rather easy to take in. What he thought he saw in my throat I can't imagine, but he's off and away fixing an appointment for me to see a specialist pal of his!' and that made her and Noel laugh some more.

Terror wrapped Judy in its folds, though she couldn't have said what was scaring her so. And then, as the woman beside her started peeling off the queer flowing shabby garments that had belonged to the late Miss Remington, and then peeled off the untidy hair and toss the wig on the back seat, Judy knew. 'Why, you're the nurse on the train!'

The other nodded. 'Yes, I never thought we'd pull it off. I must be a better actress than I gave myself credit for. Unless you're a bigger fool than I took you for!' but Noel broke in, 'Can it, Mae!' so the other woman said no more. Then followed a very unpleasant ten minutes for Judy. Her thoughts tumbled about in chaos, as she realised that her own instinctive feelings were right and that this could not possibly be Miss Banford, although the doctor and his mother were quite sure that it was. They had given away no end of information to her — and to the other side — and her own feelings about the man in the zippered jacket hadn't been wrong, either. Of course he was an enemy. Everything in her had shrieked it, and now, if she had wanted a fact to prove it, there was that statement Miss Banford had made to the doctor and his mother, that she had engaged this man in the jacket to watch Judy after she had gone to the house and discovered her aunt was dead. Judy now recalled that this same man had been following her about in Southgrove since the day Miss Remington had died.

They came to a halt at the traffic lights and Judy made a lightning movement to open the window by her and lean out, but the woman's hands were on her, and as David had discovered, she had a hard and strong grip. Judy screamed 'Help!' but as if anticipating it, Noel roared the car enough to drown her cry and nobody standing about appeared to notice, although this was a busy part of

Southgrove town. Judy let herself be pulled back on the seat, and the woman leaned forward and wound up the window. 'Don't do that again,' she said in a low menacing voice.

'But where are you taking me? My friends will bring the police — ' Judy began, but this only elicited more laughter.

'Oh, Judy, haven't you discovered by now that everyone thinks you're a crank with a flair for tall and very improbable stories?' Noel drawled. 'Now, in case you would like to save us time later, what did you do with them?'

'Them?' Judy echoed, stupefied with the truth of what he had just said. The utter, unarguable truth. Even David's friend, the police sergeant, no longer wanted to hear what Judy had been saying.

'Them. The little packets you found all over the place in the late Miss Remington's house,' Noel reminded her.

Now Judy was desperate. 'Oh, the

packets of drugs! Well, of course I know what was in them *now*, since your friend here told David and his mother what they were!'

She heard Noel draw in his breath and mutter something like 'You fool!' but Judy was mainly concerned with the stinging blow aimed at her by the woman beside her, a blow that made her see stars. '*I* didn't say that — the doctor said *you* told him that, and lying to us now won't get you anywhere!'

Judy gathered her forces. 'Well, I really couldn't understand why you told them so much, if you weren't Miss Banford,' and the woman laughed nastily and said, 'I didn't tell them anything. I merely appeared to be giving information, to make them *think* I was Miss Banford, just as I made you think on the train that I was a nurse in fear of my life. And you did!'

'How did they make me think they had thrown you off the train?' Judy asked, through swollen lips, but she did so badly want to know.

'It was easy. You were a gift from heaven. I shrieked enough, and someone held you from behind and while you looked round at him, the boys lowered me to the ground and I crawled away behind them to the next compartment, while they were looking out of the window to see how far they'd thrown me. And you revelled in it, didn't you? What you called them!'

'Why didn't anyone admit seeing a nurse?' Judy asked wearily, wondering how she could have been such a gullible idiot on that journey that day.

'Because they didn't see a nurse, dear. I pulled my felt hat off and all they saw was a girl with a lot of blonde hair and a dark coat. Men always look at blonde hair and I was lucky — almost all men in the other compartment that day!' And then they pulled up outside of a house in a narrow dark street of terraced dwellings that looked unsavoury to say the least. Noel remarked, 'We don't seem to have got our answer, so we shall have to try persuasion, shan't we? And do keep your mouth shut, Mae!'

Then he saw Judy's bruised face. 'Good heavens, did you have to do that so soon?' he asked.

'Oh, that's all right,' Mae said cheerfully. 'I can go a lot harder a bit later on, if she doesn't tell us what we want to know.'

Judy was bundled into the house. It was ill-lit and smelt of dampness and stale cooking. Other people moved about in the shadows. She saw packing cases and a rickety table, on which was a candle. Apparently this was a house that was supposed to be empty, with all the services cut off. Her heart beat faster as she realised what was going to happen to her. This, she guessed, was a street going down to the river. One of the streets Miss Remington had warned her about, after dark. Miss Remington had had a great fear of thugs and the snatching of handbags; the ills and crimes and low life of her beloved town, and that made it unsavoury for a young girl to be alone in, after dark. And Noel as an escort hadn't appealed to Miss Remington really, Judy remembered. Had Miss Remington a premonition of what was going to happen, or just an in-built dislike of someone like Noel? And try as she would, Judy couldn't think of him as anything but Noel. That had been the name he had said was his, she remembered indignantly, that first day he had come to Mrs. Venny's and told her that they must see more of each other. And all the time he was signing into Mrs. Venny's visitor's book as Mike Nolan. Why, why? And how many other names had he got?

Now they were asking her, over and over again, where the packets were that she had found, and each time she said she hadn't got them or didn't know where they were, Mae hit her, until her face and head felt like a sponge.

At last, when her mouth was so swollen, that nothing seemed to matter much more, Judy put a question herself, to Noel: 'What happened to the

Frabham diamond necklace, Noel? The one you took!'

It was a thoroughly loaded question, which made two things happen. Noel himself sprang at her, like a tiger, although up till now he had been sitting composedly enough watching Mae hitting Judy. And Mae fell on Noel, dragging his hands off Judy's throat and twisting one arm behind him in a way that made him scream. Mae was certainly talented, Judy thought bitterly.

Mae said, 'The Frabham haul, eh? And you let us think it was rubbish, *she'd* switched for the dope! Ah, well, this line of questioning has certainly brought out something, hasn't it, chum?' and she called to someone called Bert, and someone called Tiny, who was inevitably a slow lumbering giant of a man. 'Now then,' Mae purred, 'Tell us what you know about the Frabham diamonds,' she said to Judy, 'and we might just let you go. We can find the other things we lost.'

'They were in that packet he gave me

to take to London,' Judy said wearily, which was as true as anything she could have told them. Mae, however, got so angry at that, that Tiny held her off Judy.

Tiny had a strange light-weight high voice for such a big man. He advised Judy, 'Don't tease her, lass. Can't take teasing, our Mae. Never could. Besides we borrowed that packet off you, didn't we, and there wasn't nothing much in it. Unless there was another packet you forgot to mention?'

His soft voice mislead her. Judy screamed in agony as he twisted her arm.

'Look, you can do what you like to me, but you can't make me know something I've never known. Noel wanted me to persuade Miss Remington to sign documents, he was there at the top of the stairs when she was dead at the bottom and I let myself in, and he phoned me to take a packet to someone in Hatton Garden and bought my ticket for the train. That's all I know.'

'Liar!' Mae screamed and hit her so hard that Judy fainted.

When she came to she didn't open her eyes for the moment. Her whole head felt as if it had swollen to twice its size and she had the hazy notion that her eyes were open but so swollen that she couldn't see. People were talking near at hand; quarrelling, rather. Noel, trying to justify himself, and the others shouting at him. It seemed to Judy that none of them knew where the diamond necklace was, not even Noel, but the others hadn't known he was in No. 17, or that he had had any hand in Miss Remington's death. Apparently he had been sent there to pick up the packets he had been systematically hiding there. Dope, it seemed to Judy, was a dangerous thing to have to store, because of the tendency of the police to make raids. Nobody had suspected the house of an untidy cluttered old lady who lived alone with two cage birds, two old cats loathed by the neighbourhood and a bad-tempered fat old Peke.

It was a perfect cover. But Noel had also taken part (or so it seemed to Judy) in a country house robbery and had somehow acquired part of the spoils, and he had hidden that, too, in No. 17. Judy thought dazedly that that assertion on the part of the bogus Miss Banford that the idol had no secret drawer in it, should have told them all that she was not the niece of Miss Remington, for Judy herself had gathered, in her first week with Miss Remington, that all these Eastern trophies had been sent to her by her niece, although at the time Miss Remington hadn't referred to her as her niece, but as Miss Frances Banford, the inveterate globe trotter, in such a tone as to suggest that Miss Remington despised such a person for not staying at home. But she had made no secret of the fact that Frances Banford had sent them and Frances Banford had disclaimed to the doctor that she had no knowledge of the secret drawer. Carrying their discrediting of Judy herself too far? Or did she really not know about it? Judy was inclined, even in her pain-filled state, to suspect the latter.

She lay half awake, half unconscious. Sometimes she slipped down into the darkness, and dreamed. Sometimes she was awake and hearing them quarrelling. The row swayed this way and that. Sometimes Mae was on Noel's side, sometimes against him. When she was against him she was inclined to think he had somehow acquired the Frabham necklace and was using their hiding-place — Miss Remington's house — for his share of the robbery. Sometimes she was good naturedly unable to accept that he had had the shrewdness to either acquire stolen gems or to know where to hide them. She laughed at the thought of a secret drawer in the base of an idol, and then she became suspicious and was sure he had taken their spoils, made off with the lot.

She had the warped jealousy that was bad for their plans; she agreed when the others reminded her that Noel had been told to cultivate Judy just because she happened to be the one working in the house at the time, yet she swayed and was sure that Noel was infatuated with Judy and had perhaps agreed to share the spoils of both the Frabham necklace and the dope with her. And so it swayed, first to Noel, then against him, and towards the end Mae had managed to persuade the rest of them that Noel had cheated them all.

Judy must have been out for a long time. When she came to someone was shaking her. The world outside was deadly quiet, except for a couple of cats fighting, their ghastly howls rising to the moon, which shone through the dirty uncurtained windows. 'Tiny' was the one shaking her, and as his most gentle movement was like a giant's touch, she was promptly sick and he swore. But he calmed down, clumsily mopped at her face with something the size of a tablecloth, and intimated hoarsely to her that he was not like the others. He had the 'savvy' to know that she knew nothing, and because he didn't want to be part of a killing, which wasn't, he assured, his line, he proposed to let her free.

She couldn't believe it. She felt too ill to grapple with the thought, too ill to be even suspicious. She let Tiny yank her to her feet, half pushing half pulling her to the door, which he softly opened and thrust her out. She fell to the ground, so with a muttered imprecation, he picked her up, and set her on her feet, walking her along with his arm round her, until the night air had partially revived her, and by that time they had left the dark and narrow street and reached the light thoroughfare. Here, Tiny said, with realism, he must leave her.

She stood swaying. She wanted to run, before the others discovered her absence. But to run was impossible. It was as much as she could do to stand.

Someone came up to her and said something. It wasn't a policeman, so she just stared back, and wondered what she ought to do. She had no coat, her bag was heaven knew where, and nothing she had could persuade a taxi to take her to Axwood, she was quite sure. But the woman who was at her elbow was kindly, and coming to the wrong deductions, took her to yet another hovel, swearing all the way about the objectionable habits of men, all men. Judy let the woman bathe her face, pour scalding liquid down her throat and lay her on some sort of a rumpled bed.

The idea had been Bert's, to let Judy free. The boss, he said, would be coming soon. Better let Judy go free and follow her. She would lead them to the things they had lost, and then they would be in a position to face the Boss when he arrived. The Boss was not the leader of the dope ring. They didn't know who that was. The Boss was the area head, a sinister little man whose soft voice struck real fear into their hearts, and whose idea of punishment made theirs look juvenile and inept. Mae and Noel stopped their quarrelling and agreed with Bert. Bert was also the one detailed to follow Judy, and he was considerably put out to see where she had been taken.

So he got ready to wait. He waited in a doorway until it was light. Refreshed with sleep and the woman's idea of liquid restorative, Judy left her wristwatch by way of the only payment she had on her. The woman was in a torpor of sleep, so Judy tottered out, but found she could walk better this morning. But a sight of her battered face in a doorway made her chary of the stares of strangers. With a frightened flutter of the heart, she wondered where she could go, and remembered Miss Remington's doctor, the only person connected with that lady who would be available at this hour of the day.

What was his name, she tried to jerk her fuddled brain into movement. Dr. Ferne, that was it. Somehow, forcing one leg before another, and avoiding any other human being, though the working world in this district was fast ejecting itself from its sleeping places into the daylight, she found the street, and his surgery. Somehow she got to the door and rang the bell, but it was the day bell and rang unceasingly and to no avail. She tried the night bell, and fetched the doctor down, bleary-eyed, in his dressing-gown. 'Good God!' he said, at sight of her, and pulled her in.

'What happened to you? Road accident? I'll get an ambulance.'

'No, no, I — I ran into something,' she was shocked to hear herself say. 'I couldn't think who else to ask because I've lost my bag. I want to get home.'

'Where's home?' he demanded, tenderly examining her face. 'You've been beaten up. Who did it?'

She shrugged. 'I believe it's called 'mugging',' and he nodded, satisfied. Why court more derision and disbelief by telling the truth, which after all would sound only like one of her regular tall stories? This was bringing its own conviction in its trail by the doctor's next words; 'Aye, well, this'll be one thing I can believe! Oh, yes, I've heard what you've been telling poor old Wardlaw. What made you tell such wild stories? Holes in the attic walls indeed. You couldn't get in the house to see — Wardlaw's sensibly had a new lock put on the door. Did you know that? I told him to do it. That fool of a clerk of his wouldn't have such an idea.'

I bet he wouldn't, Judy thought, and wondered why Mae had said, in her guise of Miss Banford, that the solicitor's clerk was in it too. True or false? She gave up the weary tangle and winced as he painted her face with something he assured her he did for any other mugging case, of which the district had many. 'And now I suppose I'll have to ring for a taxi for you.'

Something in her face, perhaps the beaten look in her eyes, and the fear that lurked there, made him say, 'Oh, well, you look all in. Wait while I get some clothes on and we'll have a bit of breakfast together, and then if you can bring yourself to tell me a truthful story, I'd like to know what you were doing in this town after dark. Asking for a mugging, I'd say.'

To tell the truth to this little realist of a man was untold luxury. While she waited for him, Judy pondered over what she would say to him. In the end, however, she said nothing, because there was nothing in her story of the things that had really happened to her, and the way they had happened as explained by Mae, that Judy could reasonably tell Dr. Ferne. He would never believe her.

He had done a lightning job of shaving and dressing, although he still managed to look as if he'd been at a party all night. He said, 'I've got my housekeeper up. She'll have eggs and ham for us in no time. You'd like that, eh? Not slimming, are you?' to which Judy first nodded, then shook her head.

'Well,' he said, 'I'm not the deaf one — that's my housekeeper — so talk, girl. Make it worth my while abandoning any attempts to go back to sleep.'

'What can I tell you, Dr. Ferne? If I

said Miss Remington had been murdered, you'd never believe me.'

'No, I wouldn't, and none of those clown's tricks in this house, my girl! You can pull the wool over that young doctor's eyes if you like. Oh, I heard the shindy he caused when he went to see poor old Wardlaw. What are you doing — working as maid or receptionist to this young chap?'

'Receptionist,' Judy said. It was easier than to try to explain how David had taken her in off that train that day and been kind to her or that his mother had taken so kindly to David's idea of keeping Judy sheltered from the world. Dr. Ferne would think David was an idiot, too.

'Receptionist. Um, pity, I thought I might have been able to persuade you to take home with you this damned bird of Miss Remington's. Keeps calling for you, but maybe that was just mocking the old lady. I imagine she was calling you all the time, eh?' and Judy nodded.

The bird. Why should it call for her? She said, without quite knowing why, 'I'll take it, if you like. Dr. Marland's mother likes birds in cages.'

He looked really pleased. 'She does? Well, take it with my blessing. Perhaps I'll get a bit of peace. Funny, these old ladies liking birds in cages.' Judy resisted the temptation to tell him Mrs. Marland wasn't old at all. He went on, 'My housekeeper's different, though. Doesn't like cleaning them out. Hasn't cleaned the cage since it came. Told her it wasn't hygenic. The budgies died, you know. Perhaps you'd better take their cage as well. Your Mrs. Thingummy might want to put two new budgies in it. Yes, that's the ticket!' he said, getting hastily to his feet though his breakfast was only half-eaten, for the telephone was ringing.

The telephone. It's sound chilled her. Judy's heart thumped, uneasily. She had the wild unreasoning feeling that it would be someone asking if she was there, someone belonging to Mae and

Noel. This doctor wouldn't have the sense to say she wasn't. She held her breath, but she needn't have worried. It was a patient.

'Damn, can't wait to finish that,' he said, looking regretfully at the eggs, sausages and bacon, and the lavish rack of toast awaiting him. 'Eat what you want before you go, though. No need for you to rush,' he thought to tell Judy, so she thanked him, and asked him to tell his housekeeper to hand her the cages. He said vaguely he would, packing his bag at top speed, and then she was alone.

Somehow he had made the housekeeper understand she was to relinquish the mynah bird and the other cage. Perhaps because it was what the woman wanted, she had bothered to try and understand. She even smiled at Judy and asked if she should get her a taxi. Judy, remembering she was deaf, mouthed the word: 'How?' The housekeeper pointed cheerfully out of the window. The baker's van was there. 'He'll whistle one up,' she said.

The baker's man, the one who had given her a lift recently. A man she could trust. Would it be better to ask him for a lift? But the housekeeper was already on her way to take in the bread and ask him to whistle up a cab.

She made him understand, it was clear, for he glanced at the door to see who the fare would be, and then he recognised Judy.

'I'll take you, lass, if you're not in a hurry!' he shouted.

Judy's heart sank. That's right, tell all the street it's me. Already she had seen a man who looked suspiciously like Bert, or was she imagining things again? The baker was busy shouting greetings at her, inviting her to step into the van and make herself comfortable while he delivered nearby. The mynah bird was going mad, shouting, 'It's Judy! Judy! Come and take a walk, dear! Look under me cage! Don't be a fool! Murder, murder! Look under me cage, dear!'

The housekeeper came back. 'He'll

get you a cab, dear,' she said, with the impossibly bland smile of the deaf who had no idea of what verbal chaos was going on around them. Judy's exploring fingers under the bird's cage found the thing which would be the end of it all. Stuck to the base was a packet . . .

★   ★   ★

Nightmares had never been like this. Nightmares could never be as bad as this, Judy felt. Here was the baker at the door, and at the bottom, near his van stood Bert, waiting . . . for what? And beyond the van, on the far side of the road, stood Noel, for good measure. So they had let her out to follow her. Another frame-up. They knew she wouldn't call the police, or if she did, the police would never believe her. Caught, caught . . .

'Gawd, what happened to your face, miss?' She said to the baker, 'A party! Never again! Will you do something for me? Very special? Take the bird to Mrs.

Marland. And don't let anything happen to him. She's very fond of birds.' And all the while she was talking she was levering the package off the base of the cage. Not too difficult since the medical plaster was already peeling off. The baker said, 'Well, I dunno, miss,' then decided he would, 'You want to go back by cab, that's it, I suppose?' and he grinned. Hide that face he was thinking.

'I don't think there's room for the bird *and* me, and I want to phone Mrs. Marland first and warn her what's coming.' And he understood that.

'I'll take the other cage too, shall I?' he thought to come back and ask.

Now she was exposed to view in the doorway. No sense in hiding. Something prompted her to clutch the empty cage to her, as if it were precious, and to shake her head. The baker, laughing, went off with the mynah bird.

Feeling sick with apprehension, Judy hastily dialled the Marlands' number, and prayed that it wouldn't be engaged.

Mrs. Marland answered. 'Judy! Where are you? We've been crazy with worry! David's here . . . '

David shouted down the telephone, 'Judy, where are you? Concise instructions, please!'

What did he think she'd tell him, for heaven's sake? She shut her eyes. The bread was in, the housekeeper closing the door. They would be there, waiting for her to go out to that cab. She said to David, 'I'm in danger. At the moment I'm in Dr. Ferne's house, Faddon Street, Southgrove. But there's a cab been ordered, and they're waiting to get me . . . Noel, all his people. David, bring your friend the sergeant, *please* . . . '

David said, 'Damn the cab! Stay there in that house. Tell that fool of a housekeeper not to let anyone in. You hear me?'

She said yes, and promised, but it wasn't any use. She heard the cab arrive. The housekeeper was looking out for it, and wouldn't be stopped from opening the door. She just wouldn't understand that Judy now didn't want to go. The cab driver made the same ejaculation as the baker on seeing her face. For a moment Judy thought he was going to refuse to accept her as a fare. Then when he saw Noel and Bert moving in, he did refuse. 'Now look, miss, I don't want no rough-house in my cab ... ' and he was gone, but not before Bert had ripped up the steps and got a foot in the door. Judy threw her weight against it. The empty bird cage banged metallically against the door, possibly making Bert think a barricade was being put up. He held off to take a mighty lunge at the door and gave Judy time to shut it. She put up the chain and breathed again, briefly. The housekeeper, happy now that the mynah bird had gone, and even the noisesome empty cage of the dead budgies, kicked and banged cheerfully in the kitchen and sang off key at her work — 'Some day my prince will come', she trilled, clashing crockery, and supremely unaware that Bert and Noel were raining blows on the front door.

The back door, Judy's mind hammered. She quietly went through, the housekeeper's back was turned as she hung up a frying pan she had been scouring and was completely unaware that Judy hadn't taken the cab she had procured for her. Judy ran down the garden and out of the back door into an alley and prayed that Noel and Bert wouldn't think of this too.

Noel had. He was there, sprinting after her, and she was holding the packet that had been stuck to the bottom of the cage. She was in no state for running. She ducked into a shop and hid behind a fat woman staring at some bacon but Judy's face aroused comment wherever she went. She saw Noel streak past so she slipped out again and ran back the other way. She should have gone upstairs and hidden in the doctor's house. Or shut herself in the loo until David came. Why hadn't she thought of that? Because, came the answer, in their present mood Noel and Bert would have battered down any door long before that.

Desperation seized her. One week, one day before that, and she would never have thought of creeping into a waiting van and hiding on the floor of the cab while she got her second wind. Noel came back and converged with Bert, and they talked about where she could be. 'She's near here. She was in no state for running,' Noel panted. Neither was he very fit for running, she thought, and as she lay there, she looked at the packet. It was addressed to her. Miss Judy Henderson, it said. She closed her eyes. If only she had a pen, she could put the doctor's address on it and mark it urgent and post it. She could see a letterbox. It would get there and all that would be required would be surcharge on it. And there, at hand, was the driver's delivery board and his stylo. She reached for it, and wrote in block capitals the words URGENT FOR DR. MARLAND, and his address underneath it.

And then the driver of the van

returned. He was the same height and build as 'Tiny' with a hideously cheerful face and great hands like hams. The cheerful look slipped a bit as he saw the face of the girl crouching on the floor of his van, but his intelligence didn't rise to keeping quiet about her presence. 'What the — happened to your kisser?' he boomed picturesquely, so Judy, to the last ends of desperation, raised herself and peeped over the edge of the windscreen, and Noel and Bert turning at the sound of the voice, and said, 'Those two men did it. Just because I wanted to post this, private and personal and special,' and she ended by holding up the packet.

The van driver swore so colourfully then that Judy, who didn't understand half the words, reddened just the same. The implication was there. 'Them two?' he asked, and strolled over to Noel and Bert, who couldn't believe what was going to happen to them until it was too late, far too late. The van driver quietly knocked their heads together, watched them fall in an untidy heap before the startled eyes of a bystander, dusted his hands and came back to Judy. 'Out you get, gel. Go and post your packet. Another time we'll have a ball, you and me, but you ain't in no condition for larks right now, eh?' and he lifted her down as easily as if she were a baby, and the playful push he gave her towards the letterbox made her head reel for the moment.

But she got her packet posted, and she could now go back to the doctor's house and wait for David, who should be arriving about now.

Afterwards, David could do nothing but blame himself, but it had seemed the best thing to do, at the time, for his friend the sergeant had now really listened to him, on the strength of Judy's being missing. They had thrown out a net over Southgrove, and had been lucky in finding two of the gang again searching No. 17 Highview Crescent and the neighbouring attics. One of the men got away, but other police followed him back to the mean street where Judy had been held, and caught the others. Just a handful of the lowest level of the dope ring, but it was a start. It had been the fact that they had had no lead at all, which had worried the police so much. But they found nothing.

And then Judy had telephoned Mrs. Marland, with the address where she was, and that had changed everything. But on the way to the house with his friend the sergeant, in a police car, David had heard a police call over the radio, about the body of a Miss Jones, the elderly typist of a local solicitor, being found dead at the foot of her fire stairs. Her flat had been ripped to pieces, including a cat basket, and the two old cats had escaped, neighbours said, at the time of sounds of a fight.

David remembered. The combination of cats, cat basket, and the fact that the dead woman was the employee of Mr. Wardlaw, and had taken Miss Remington's cats, was more than enough. They stopped at her flat on the way.

Neighbours were horrified. Miss Jones liked to keep herself to herself, they said, and besides, she was always having thrillers on her TV set, and it only sounded like the usual shouting and bumping about. Then it had all gone suddenly quiet, but nobody had thought at the time that anything was wrong. They were by then watching their own TV sets, or going to bed.

But the visit to that flat had made David late for picking up Judy, who he thought would be safely within the doctor's house in Faddon Street. The housekeeper, when she could at last be contacted, opened the door for them and wasted a lot of time by telling them she was deaf. She did, however, lip-read, a fact which Judy hadn't known, and she told them with a long-winded pleasure, that she knew when the front door bell rang if she happened to be facing the contraption the doctor had had fixed up in each room. A doll danced on the end of a wire when the bell was ringing. She was so pleased to be able to tell them that. And no, the young lady had gone off in a taxi, some time ago. The baker had got the taxi for her, and she had taken away that horrible old black bird in its cage and the nasty second cage which had had the budgies in it.

David looked dreadful. The sergeant said, 'Thought of something?' and David said, 'Yes, a thing I should have thought of long before. That bird kept calling for Judy. Somewhere in that cage was the missing things. There couldn't be any other place where the old lady could have hidden them.'

'The packets of dope? In a bird cage?' The sergeant wasn't impressed with that idea. But David said, 'Not just the packets of dope. Remember there's a missing diamond necklace worth heaven knows how much.'

The sergeant was about to look disbelieving, as by habit, when Judy's assertions were mentioned, but David said fiercely, 'We now know there was a necklace missing, don't we, from some other robbery? What's to prevent one of the gang from hiding it along with the other stuff?'

'Form,' the sergeant said clearly. 'Dope peddlars aren't country house robbers and vice versa.' He shook his head. 'Don't say 'could be' because it's a well-known fact that every criminal sticks to his own line.'

David telephoned his mother. 'Is Judy back yet? She took a cab!'

His mother said, 'No, David, but something queer is going on. She gave the mynah bird in its cage to the baker's man to deliver here. She said it was important. She was going to stay in the doctor's house. Isn't she there?'

'No, Mother! That's where I am and that's why I'm telephoning you. What's so special about the baker delivering the bird? Damned smart of Judy to give it to him!'

'Well, I don't think it is and he certainly doesn't. He was beaten up and his van overturned, and the bird and the cage were found not far away. The bird was killed and the cage had a place where something had been stuck to the bottom. Oh, David, what's happened to Judy?'

David replaced the receiver. His worst fears showed plainly in his face as he recounted his mother's half of the conversation to the sergeant. 'They've got Judy,' he said, 'and they've got what was under the cage. But what was it? Dope or . . . the necklace?'

★   ★   ★

The van driver kept on wondering about Judy. His thinking processes were slow, but his hands were gentle on the wheel of his beloved van. That was his life, his van. He kept it running so sweetly for his firm. He wished it was his. Next he liked frail little girls like Judy and wished she had been his. It would have given him much pleasure to punish every other man who looked at her, let alone beat her up. He hadn't enjoyed knocking out Bert and Noel because it had been over so quickly. He ought to have gone back and waited for them to recover and given them some more. He ought, he thought belatedly, to have crept along behind that frail little girl, to see that no other people molested her. He should have asked where she was going, given her a lift home. She looked none too steady on her pins, come to think of it.

He delivered his last parcel and turned the van to retrace his path from where he had left Judy. But neither Judy nor the two men were to be seen. Remnants of the crowd which had hastily formed to watch proceedings, were just trickling away, so disappointed, he drove back to his works, to pick up more deliveries. On the way a police barrier required him to stop and answer questions. Always inclined to be belligerent with police enquiries, he was inclined to say he had never seen either the two men or Judy, even though the police suggested that many people had described him and his van and what had happened.

David happened to be near, talking to the sergeant, and heard this. David's enquiry, coupled with the information that he was a friend of hers, and a doctor, soothed the angry van driver enough for him to say plaintively, 'Well, all she wanted was to post her little packet. That's all! But they wouldn't let her! So I knocked their (something) heads together so she could get to the pillar box.'

David breathed a deep sigh of relief, Bless her, she'd got one packet, at least, and had thought of the one safe way of getting it to him! But where was she now? He said so, which aroused more fury in the van driver, to think that the frail little girl was missing, after being beaten up, and all her man-friend could do was to stand at a police barrier talking with the sergeant. As soon as they released him, he turned his van back into Southgrove. The only way he knew how to search for someone was to keep driving, keep looking . . .

By that time Noel had recovered enough from his knockout blow by the van driver, to go back to where he had left his car. He now knew enough of Judy's tricks to know that to follow her on foot was disastrous. Tired she may be, beaten up and still suffering a certain amount of shock, but she seemed to have limitless friends in vans; bakers' deliveries and for all he knew, chaps in big cars. But if he drove slowly enough along the road she had taken, the chances were she would slip out of a shop where she had hidden behind other customers as she had done earlier today.

That way he found her. In her present exhausted state it wasn't difficult to jerk her back into the car, and passers by merely thought it was an irate husband, the way he snapped: 'Judy! Do you have to be all day in the shops? Where am I supposed to park?'

It was such a pity, she could have cried — she was so near Fadden Street. It was only on the next corner. And now he had got her again and to judge from what 'Tiny' had said, the whole gang's intentions were lethal now, and Noel was one of the gang. A fact she still found it hard to take in.

He said, 'You really are a pest, you know! All I wanted was a little time, and if you'd done as I said, and not gone screaming to strangers like the Marlands, you and I could have taken the stuff and the diamonds and blown the lot and had thousands to spend! Abroad somewhere, where it was safe! And now you've ruined everything!'

As she said nothing, he snarled, 'You aren't even listening to me!'

'Why should I bother,' she said tiredly. 'I don't suppose you need my services any longer, and I gather I am expendable.'

'No, love, not yet,' he said softly. 'We've got the stuff. Now we just want the Frabham necklace. If you're a good girl and tell me where it is, you and I could still cash it and live comfortably on the proceeds. Come *on*, Judy, where is it?'

She said, in such genuine surprise that he was almost tempted to believe her, 'If you've got the one, you've got the other! They were together, surely!' For it struck her that the packet must surely contain the dope, too. They were such tiny packs she had kept finding in Miss Remington's rooms, and she had read before that such a little amount would fetch fantastic prices because the need for the stuff made people pay such high prices for it. 'How did you find it, anyway?'

'You don't listen to the radio, do you, and I do. Those damned cats! Real clever of the old girl to hide the dope in their basket, wasn't it?'

'What are you talking about?' Judy asked, still in that blank surprise.

Noel thought fast. They hadn't found the dope, though that Jones woman, he had just heard in a radio news flash, had been found dead. How the others would carry on; murder, and still nothing found! And what would the Boss have to say? Like the others, he feared the sinister soft-spoken little man who had the habit of raising an eye-lid which meant the termination of someone's life in the gang for sheer inability to do what the Boss wanted. It didn't matter if the task was impossible or the person merely inefficient. Death followed, sometimes a nasty death. Without thinking, Noel had driven slowly down to the wharves and he brought the car to a standstill.

Judy was staring at him with horror. 'You killed her? Well, your friends did? That nice inoffensive old secretary who never did any harm to anyone but take the old cats in, so they shouldn't be sent to be put down! And you killed her? Why, why? She knew nothing about anything!'

'Then you tell me where the stuff is, because you haven't got it in your room and it isn't in your room at the Marlands and I just don't see where it could be unless it's on you somewhere,' and he let his eyes rove over her slender body in the way he used to, when he could make her almost choke with the breathlessness of anticipation mixed with fear, because of the savagery of his love-making when he was not pleased. He was not pleased now . . . but since then Judy had met David, and she knew now that nothing Noel could do could arouse any emotion in her except to utterly repel her.

'You won't find anything,' she said, in a stifled voice, 'because its all in official hands, and you might as well take me back for all the good it will do you.'

Such an ugly look came over his face that it jerked some energy into her tired limbs. She was out of the car before he realised her intentions. This was not the Judy he used to know, the girl who was easy to handle. She looked round for a startled second, assessing the way to go, rather like an animal at the chase, taking the right road through sheer desperation. She eschewed the way they had come; it was a cobbled lane going uphill. She shot down towards the edge of the water.

It was slippery on the stones. Narrow where it ran to the wharf edges, and there were hanging chains, from the open doors above where goods were lowered down to the boats. Nothing had been modernised in Southgrove; they found they could jog along nicely in their own small way. Desultory work was going on at the next wharf but nobody was looking at her. They were watching a bale swinging against the sky, shouting up that it was insufficiently secured by its ropes. Judy hesitated, and Noel was on her like a tiger. He pushed her back in the doorway of the first wharf, shadowed, silent, with only a watchman at the far end, who thought they were a young couple skylarking. He returned to his inspection of the piles of bales and didn't see Noel's hands on Judy's throat.

'Now, Judy, what's got into you? Let's put cards on the table, shall we? Okay, I set it up on the train for you and you behaved very nicely. Smart girl to pull the communication cord. It added a nice touch of authenticity to it all. Only why didn't you let them ship you to hospital?'

'Hospitals full up,' she gasped, and again surprised that ugly look on his face, this time because Fate had stepped in and spoiled his plan.

'How come the wrong necklace got in that damned drawer in the idol?' he demanded, releasing her throat enough for her to answer.

'I don't know, I don't know. It was a different one Miss Remington showed me!' Judy said, but he pounced on that. 'So you've got the real one!' He looked savagely down into Judy's bruised young face and said, between his teeth, 'An old fool of a spinster living in a house of rubbish, and a stupid girl with a silly voice, and you both fooled me! That old woman must have passed it to you somehow, and she insisted to the last that she hadn't got the real thing and didn't know where it was!'

'You killed her!' Judy had to believe it now. 'You killed Miss Remington!'

'I didn't, but I would have done if she

hadn't moved back and gone down the stairs. I never have any luck. If you hadn't come back for those damned cats, you wouldn't have been prowling about and I'd have seen that necklace in the Buddha's drawer wasn't the real thing. Then *they* found it!'

'They expected the dope to be in that packet?' Judy asked, remembering the crowd of young men round that nurse. Well, they had looked like young men at first, but Bert must have been one of them, and 'Tiny' might well have been the one who did the mock 'throwing out of the window' act. It had been a lot of men to her startled eyes.

Something moved near them. A huge shadow, the hulk of a big man. Judy's hopes of escape fell to zero now, for this must be 'Tiny' come to help Noel. Noel undoubtedly thought so, too. He said, 'She hasn't got it. No joy here!'

The huge man came out the shadows but it wasn't Noel's friend. It was Judy's friend, the van driver, who had come right through from the other end.

With a roar he sprang at Noel, for having his hands at Judy's throat. Judy was flung to one side, and almost went over the edge into the water. Noel, slick as ever, dodged the heavy bulk of his adversary, and jumped over Judy's body, with the intention of running past the crowd of men trying to manoeuvre the big bale whose weight was still not by any means safely fixed. Their anxious warning shouts to those up above in the opening drowned what was going on behind, but the attention of the man above was taken by Noel's dash for freedom, and they weren't paying attention to the big bale. Just as Noel ran beneath it, it fell.

It all happened so quickly that Judy was hard put to it to know exactly what had happened. The big van driver had scooped her up to set her down in the doorway of the empty wharf in safety, no doubt while he went in search of his quarry. He wanted to punish Noel. She bounded out again to see what would happen, and heard running footsteps to the right. It was David, the sergeant, and behind him two more policemen. In her glad recognition of David, and his anger at the sight of her bruised face, what was happening to Noel was lost. But the sergeant and his men saw what happened and went forward. Their bulk, and the men who had been waiting to receive the bale blotted out the broken body of Noel as it lay, half under that fallen weight.

Then David released Judy and went forward himself, as his friend the sergeant called him. After all, he was a doctor, Judy thought confusedly, as the men moved back and she saw legs and feet, and knew someone had been hurt.

She went slowly forward, impelled by heaven knew what. Noel's face was covered in blood, but he looked at her, still angry. She thought, 'He's dying, and he's still angry with me!' Noel said something that sounded to those near him like: 'All those people, all that careful planning, and you and your damned spring-cleaning ruined it all,'

304

and a trickle of blood ran from the corner of his mouth as his eyes closed.

★　★　★

At the hospital, Judy's face was treated again, and she was left in a quiet cubicle in casualty, for shock. David came in and said, 'You've given me a lot of bad moments, Judy, love. *Please* stay here till they fetch you!'

'Why will they fetch me?' she asked, in panic. 'I don't have to see him, do I? Must I?'

'Oh, heavens, no. I *am* a clumsy idiot but I didn't think you'd think of that chap,' which was as near as he could get to mentioning Noel at all. 'No, this is to see Miss Jones, the secretary who took the old cats away.'

'But she's dead too,' Judy whispered, blanching. 'So many people dead. I feel as if I had something to do with it!'

'No, dear love, you were very brave and helped everybody, and Miss Jones isn't dead.'

'But Noel said he heard she'd been killed, on the radio — a news flash.'

'Yes. Sometimes it is allowed to let people think the victim is dead, but Miss Jones didn't die. Mind you, I understand she isn't in very good shape. I'll go with you. She wants to see you.'

'Poor thing. She must have been badly hurt.'

The sergeant had wanted Miss Jones to tell Judy the good news, but David decided to tell her himself. He had to make sure she wouldn't take off to discover what had been happening, and come to some harm again. So he said quietly, 'Miss Jones, it appears, was as fond of cats as you were, and worried because they couldn't settle down. Something under the flat cushion in the bottom of the cat basket kept creaking. So she took it out, slit open the cushion and found a strong plastic envelope inside, containing lots of tiny packets.'

Judy sat up with a jerk, which made her head reel again. David gently lowered her to the flat pillow, and advised her not to do that again for a bit. 'It was the dope all right. She's a sensible woman. She realised something had been hidden there, so she sewed up the cushion again and settled the cats down to peaceful sleep. But the problem was, where to hide the thing. She hadn't been in a lawyer's office for nothing. She guessed it was a lethal possession. So she hid it, and had just cleared away all traces of her find when she had . . . visitors.'

'Oh.' Judy closed her eyes. 'Did they knock her about too?'

'No. She got out of the window,' he said, and it was as well her eyes were closed so she couldn't see his face, as he recalled how she had got all those bruises. 'Unfortunately she caught her foot as she was jumping down to the ground — they saw her body and presumed she'd died, and they set about searching the flat and making a great deal of noise while they were doing it, but they had the sense to turn the TV on so neighbours would think it was all on the TV.'

'Where . . . where did she hide the packet?' Judy asked.

'She slipped it down behind the old fashioned cistern in the loo, and took care not to disturb the cobwebs so nobody would think of looking there. And while we're on about missing packages, where did you post the diamonds, Judy?'

'Why?' she asked, fear in her eyes.

'Someone ought to be there when the postman empties that box in case there are one or two villians still hiding, that know what happened to it,' he said grimly.

Again the High Street had some excitement. Never had a policeman presided over the collecting of mail from an ordinary red letter box. The next morning they read the whole account of the recovery of the Frabham diamonds and what went on in Miss Remington's house, and the local firm of builders had a rush job to fill up certain holes in attics in Highview Crescent. But Judy was kept out of the newspapers as much as possible. It wasn't very difficult. David had been carrying about with him a Special Licence for some days, and they slipped quietly into the local Registry Office and got married, and intended to motor up to where David's sister lived, as the least likely place they would be found in for a few blessed days of peace.

Her face was still bruised, so David's mother had advised her to wear a floral cap with a short veil on which were sewn a lot of frivolous white tufts. And Judy, who never wore make-up, felt her face was wearing a mask, with a heavy application of make-up which almost hid the bruises. It was worth it, to be able to slip away, for reporters had even been lurking outside the doctor's house in the hope of getting a picture. Judy had made local news, which would give the press something to write about well into the week-end.

A photographer and reporter were outside the Registry when David and his new wife came out. 'Isn't this Miss Henderson who was instrumental in helping catch the — ' they began, but

David brushed them aside with his new wide happy smile, and said, 'Certainly not. Quite a different person!' and they escaped to his car and got away.

But at the first stop, some fifty miles from Axwood, David turned to her and said, 'I just remembered, love. I didn't formally propose to you!'

'Well, it's too late now,' Judy grinned. 'Anyway, you did sort of — at least, your mother got out of me my dread secret, that I was in love with you, and she told me you were in love with me. So I wasn't taken by surprise.'

He tried to frown. 'The only time I ever really wanted to marry someone and I didn't even remember to do it formally!'

'Never mind, you've stopped looking all anxious and I liked the way you denied I was Judy Henderson and said I was quite a different person. Because, do you know what? I *feel* a different person!'

After he had kissed her into a breathless state, he said, 'No regrets?

About anything? After all, it won't be much fun being a doctor's wife. No glamour or excitement.'

'Darling David, don't you think we've had enough excitement in the little while I've known you, to last us a lifetime?' and as he settled down to kissing her again, he murmured against her bright hair, 'You may be right. But on second thoughts, I reckon life will always be exciting, with you, love.'

We do hope that you have enjoyed reading this large print book.

Did you know that all of our titles are available for purchase?

We publish a wide range of high quality large print books including:
Romances, Mysteries, Classics
General Fiction
Non Fiction and Westerns

Special interest titles available in large print are:
The Little Oxford Dictionary
Music Book, Song Book
Hymn Book, Service Book

Also available from us courtesy of Oxford University Press:
Young Readers' Dictionary
(large print edition)
Young Readers' Thesaurus
(large print edition)

For further information or a free brochure, please contact us at:
Ulverscroft Large Print Books Ltd.,
The Green, Bradgate Road, Anstey,
Leicester, LE7 7FU, England.
Tel: (00 44) **0116 236 4325**
Fax: (00 44) **0116 234 0205**

Other titles in the
Linford Romance Library:

SECOND CHANCE WITH THE PLAYBOY

Charlotte McFall

At thirty, Annabel Simpson is the youngest doctor to take charge of a ward in the history of Oakwood Hospital. A possible closure threatens her position and spurs her into action. Organizing a charity bike ride from Brighton to Land's End seems like a good idea — until she is paired with her wayward ex, Marcus Chapman. But Marcus has changed, still grieving the loss of his daughter, and is determined to break down the barriers Annabel has erected. Can they find the courage to mend their broken hearts?

GIRL ON THE RUN

Rhonda Baxter

A job in a patent law firm is a far cry from the glamorous existence of a pop star's girlfriend. But it's just what Jane Porter needs to distance herself from her cheating ex and the ensuing press furore. In a new city with a new look, Jane sets about rebuilding her confidence — something she intends to do alone. That is, until she meets patent lawyer Marshall Winfield. But with the paparazzi still hot on Jane's heels, and an office troublemaker hell-bent on making things difficult, can they find happiness together?